AMERICAN MANIFESTO
(Star Children – Book 2)

Gary W. Babb

AMERICAN MANIFESTO
(Star Children – Book 2)

DOUBLE DRAGON

Chapter 1
(What the Hell?)

Former President Thompson came bursting into his War Room at his Florida resort and yelled, "What the hell is going on?"

The former president, normally intimidating anyway, but suddenly appearing in his lean, straight 6' 3" height, combined with his obviously stressed demeanor, radiated the impression he was not to be fucked with, and they should comply immediately. Those in the room jumped at his sudden outburst and silence floated over the already full room before Mr. Tom Canton, the presidents former National Security Advisor, said, "Well, Mr. President we are gathering lots of facts, but none of them are making any sense."

Since President Thompson had lost his reelection, which he strongly believed was stolen by a corrupt deep state, he had maintained a team of advisors, attorneys, and a large staff to reverse the election results. He was notified during the night that something horrific was taking place in the country. He immediately called in his staff to analyze the situation, and he was now ready for his first briefing.

President Thompson said, "Tell me what you know so far."

Tom Canton said, "Data is still sketchy and is still coming in, but we can provide the following: During the last 24 hours we have identified somewhere in the neighborhood of a half a million assassinations in the U.S. and almost one trillion dollars reported hacked from various wealthy individuals and organizations."

President Thompson bellowed, "No Shit! Assassinations? That many? How could that happen without us knowing anything about it? How did we not have warning of something in the wind? Hell, government can't keep secrets." After a moment of thought and suddenly wide eyed he said, "Was I hacked?"

President Thompson personally picked and appointed NSA Canton to his position as his National Security Advisor during his first term as president. Tom was not physically impressive in stature, being bald, short, and plump; but the president trusted him implicitly. If NSA Canton said something was so, then he believed him.

"No, Mr. President, you were not hacked. Ironically, only fifteen individuals that we can identify, readily identifiable as far left-wing or deep state funders, were hacked. Some of them have been totally destroyed … some even assassinated. Additionally, the assassinations were all in that far radical left-wing of politics. It almost looks like a coup. Well, I guess it is a coup, but if it is, we don't know by whom. It does, however, seems to be a conservative movement and huge, apparently a coordinated effort to take back America from the Communist."

"Crap! You know who the media and politicians will blame. Me! And you are telling me we have no idea who and how this was done? That's really hard to believe."

Tom Canton said, "I kind of have a feeling the media will be too busy trying to save themselves. There were at least 82,000 media talking heads and reporters taken out and 22 corrupted, Communist Attorneys General and Secretaries of State. The list goes on with 57,000 lawyers, 162,000 bureaucrats in every agency, 62,000 state and federal politicians, 57,000 teachers and college professors, and many, many more. All areas of government were touched, including admirals, generals, colonels, judges, even two governors."

President Thompson sat quietly, thinking, then said, "Are you telling me all those ass holes in the media I had to deal with for four years are gone?"

Tom said, "Well, not all of them, that would take fat too many assassinations, but most of the worst ones are dead or missing. Mostly all those that remain alive you would probably consider friends, or at least fair."

President Thompson said, "Hell, I can think of some of them I've thought about killing personally. Gone, you say? So, those nasty talking-heads on TV aren't out there ripping me up?"

Tom continued, "The media is mostly quiet. They are in turmoil right now with their CEOs and department heads gone. It will take them some time to get reorganized."

"I'm not sure you all grasp the complexity and logistics required of an organization that can maintain total secrecy over a communication network large enough to coordinate an assassination

7

coup of hundreds of thousands and implement it within a 24 hour window. It's massive and has never before been attempted, much less accomplished. The technical complexity is ... well, impossible. Think about the millions of people that would have to be security vetted, the communication required to inform and coordinate, background checks on the targets, choosing the targets, assigning the proper motivated assassin. The list is endless, but the coup *was* accomplished. It's unbelievable."

President Thompson looked hard at his former FBI Director Setliff then said, "Harry, are you telling me that with all your contacts and insider information networks you don't know what's going on and who is behind this?"

Former Director Setliff's actual name was Jack. Harry was a nickname Dir. Setliff's ex-wife gave him years ago; because, according to her, he looked like Clint Eastwood, tall and lean. She called him "Dirty Harry", and the name stuck among those who knew him well, which is one reason she became his Ex.

Jack shrugged and said, "I can assure you that my network was completely silent, and I have reached out to them again. They claim to know nothing. I also know this to be true, because many of them have contacted me to find out if *we* are responsible or if we know anything. It's really a strange situation."

President Thompson asked, "Well who in the world could have pulled this off so secretly? Are the Russians or Chinese capable of doing this?"

Tom Canton shook his head and said, "I seriously doubt the Russians or Chinese would have acted to cleanse our country of Communist, which is apparently what happened. And, this money hack is seriously highly technical. I don't think even our NSA could pull this off. What I'm hearing is that they can't even figure out how it was done. No. It's someone else."

President Thompson said, "Who the hell is in charge of the country right now? Is President Dufus still there?"

Tom said, "To the best of our knowledge the president and his administration are still in control. The Coup was careful to leave an operational government in place, and their reasoning is still unclear."

Jack Setliff, who had remained silent for a while, suddenly slammed his fist down on the table and bellowed, "Hell! I know who led this Coup." He sat in silence for a moment confirming his internal thoughts, then continued. "It's the Star Children. They saved us once already by utilizing high tech. I believe they are trying to save us again. Think about it. They are insanely brilliant and with their alien, Arcadian archive they have access to almost endless volumes of advanced technology. Working with them during the Alien Wars and afterwards I was privy to their technical abilities and potentials. They could easily pull this off if they desired. But what I'm having trouble accepting are the assassinations, the taking of human lives, certainly on this scale, seems utterly uncharacteristic for them. The Arcadians were and are, in their genetically modified Star Children form, a benevolent race. They would not normally want to harm humans."

Tom Canton was nodding as Jack spoke, and when he finished Tom said, "Yes, I agree. In fact they are probably the only group capable of doing this."

President Thompson said, "I think maybe you are right, but why would they keep it a secret from us?"

Dir. Setliff said, "They would specifically keep it a secret from us so we couldn't interfere or try to stop them. Let's not overlook the fact that total secrecy was their intended goal, and we would be consider an unnecessary risk. I'm also thinking that they would want us exactly where we are now … wondering what the hell happened."

President Thompson said, "That makes sense, but we need to know now. You both have friends at their stronghold at the Sanctuary. I suggest you ask them for a ride and go in person to find out. It looks like you two are going to Antarctica. I'm not sure what we can do about it, but it's better to know for sure. One thing though, we can't pass this information out to anyone. Let's keep their secret."

President Thompson was interrupted by his executive assistant rushing in. She quickly handed him a document. He started to read it, but after seeing the first few sentences he started over and read it aloud to the group.

American Manifesto

We are true Americans, and we are immigrants coming for the America dream and to escape Communism. We love this country and our people. "We the people" (WE) are a snake without a head. WE are millions joining together to take our country back. You can't find us, because we are a movement of millions, and WE are among you. You can't hide from us. WE know who you are by your deeds and actions, or lack of action, You will conform to the original American values as founded and guaranteed in the Constitution of the United States, or you will be purged. WE are not Globalist, Communist, anarchist, criminals or any other group dedicated to destroying America, but WE believe many of you are. WE have witnessed corruption in our country like never before seen. Criminal and corrupt activities can be seen everywhere running ramped in politics and throughout our government. The legal system is now a complete joke. Communist lawyer and judges have turned the legal system into a weapon to propagate the destruction of America. The news media is no longer a "Free Press" and is full of Fake News. It can't be trusted to tell the truth. The news media has become nothing more than propaganda for the corrupt. WE are lied to by our elected officials, who are then supported by the biased media, while the judicial systems protects them. Our citizens have no voice, and when we speak out we are silenced and attacked by our own government and the media. Up until now we have felt some marginal security by knowing our voices can still be heard through honest elections. Unfortunately, that remaining security has vanished with the last rigged election. WE watched it happen. This was the last straw for most of us. Our government can no longer be trusted, and the American people have had enough. Your rape and plunder of our country and the intimidation of WE has come to an end.

Revolution is now our only course of action, but open war with our young men and women killing each other is not acceptable. WE have decided instead to act in unison to purge the evil and corrupt individuals and organizations responsible. Read the newspapers today. WE have purged from our ranks many of those corrupt politicians, lawyers, judges, news media instigators, anarchist, bureaucrats, military leaders, and taken many sources of funding you are using for your corrupt causes. As you will soon discover, those individuals purged number in the hundreds of thousands. This is a good start, but it's only the first wave. If there are to be a second and third or more waves is completely up to you. This is your opportunity to get your act together and begin cleaning up America for "We the People". America belongs to the people. Our government is responsible for managing it for us. Get back to doing just that, or you will also be purged.

You have controlled this country, its wealth, its power, and its people with impunity far too long. Your first thoughts might be to come after us, but that would be a mistake. WE are the vast majority, and WE will be watching you, and WE are everywhere. If you come after us you will also be purged. You will join with us to make America great again, or you will be eliminated. It's just that simple.

Now, what do WE want? Understand that WE are not taking control of the government. WE will continue to allow the people to choose their leaders by honest popular vote, but WE do make the following immediate demands: There will be a general amnesty for all involved and NO investigations of any deaths occurring over the last 24 hours during our purge. WE want fair and honest elections, eliminate voting machines and go back to paper ballots, investigate and prosecute voter fraud, mandatory Voter ID, … you know the drill. Clean up our election laws to ensure and guarantee honest elections. Now, only a simpleton would believe the last election was honest. WE want the election immediately reversed and President Thompson reinstalled in office before any more damage can be done to America. If President Thompson doesn't step up to lead, WE want an immediate new election. WE want a "Free Press". WE want big tech controlled. WE want a cleansed judicial system that conforms to our Constitution. WE want our borders controlled. WE want America first.

This is your chance to get it right for America. This is your only chance. WE will be watching.

After President Thompson finished reading the Manifesto he took a deep breath and said, "I guess there is no doubt now that I will get the blame for all this. The political left and the media will crucify me. Damn!"

13

Tom Canton said, "I don't think you still fully understand the depth of this Coup. This Coup came without any warning at all and took out almost half of a million people … that's a lot of radical left-wing assassinations. I don't think the repercussions will be that bad, certainly from the media. They are decimated. All the alphabet networks, CNN, and CNBC have lost most of their standard negative and biased talking-heads and reporters. They are literally gone. Even FOX News lost the bad ones, but the good ones are still there. With the threat hanging over them of a second wave, I think they will be very slow to attack you, if at all."

"What about big tech and social media?"

"They were hit hard also, plus they lost most of their higher level executives, including some of the billionaire owners. They were also severely crippled financially by the money-hack. Their main concern for a while will be their own survival. And, before you ask, many of the far left politicians are also gone, including the Senate majority leader and the Squad. I'm not sure who would attempt to come after you at this point. Maybe we should consider going on the offensive."

President Thompson said, "Everyone will still believe I'm responsible and behind this obvious Coup."

The president's son, David, said, "You *are* responsible, father, but not the way you make it sound. You stood up to corrupt deep state and won many battles. You have inspired, motivated, and ignited the country with a movement to take back America. Now the movement has developed a life of its own. It's what we and the country needed, as drastic as it is. I say take charge of the Coup and own it." Several heads nodded around the conference table.

Director Setliff said, "Well, we can't openly own the Coup. We need to make it known that you are not responsible for the assassinations and know nothing about it; but that you understand the sentiment behind it, that it was a movement of frustration and determination by the silent majority of the country to take back our country at all cost. Let all know that you will accept the people's decisions and will lead them forward if that is their wish. Let the movement own the assassinations. Obviously they are owning that action."

"I agree with David that you need to and should now take charge of the movement and continue what the people started. Actually, if you don't, I believe the movement will clearly move forward without you. We don't want that. The vast silent majority of the country waited for someone like you to emerge for decades. Now they have it and want you to take it forward. The manifesto took total responsibility for the action and gave you an out, but they also made it clear they want you to continue to lead it. The movement is obviously committed and totally irreversible at this point. The Coup is mostly complete, and it's going forward with or without you. So, I agree, own it and lead it."

President Thompson sat in silence, thinking. He then began to smile, a smile of acceptance, and said, "This action by the movement is seriously horrific, but I do understand the necessity of it and the

15

brilliance of it. I have dreaded a revolution that appeared inevitable and unavoidable. That really was the only recourse but would have resulted in total chaos and massive loss of lives. I think this method of Coup has prevented an armed revolution. I would never have believed this possible. Yes, I will own the Coup, but realistically what can we expect now?"

It was Dr. Janet Horowitz, a constitutional scholar, that spoke, "I also agree that you should now lead the new government. I'm starting to realize that virtually all your political, legal, media, and any other opposition has disappeared. All that remains are mostly on your side of the spectrum. Only the brainwashed and duped in the population will question you, but when things turn around they will quickly come to your side. This is a perfect storm."

Dr. Horowitz was a knowledgeable and gifted speaker, having argued before the Supreme Court many times, but she was notorious for her exaggerated body language and animated movements. She was short and feisty, and at one time sported a bush of fiery-red hair on her head to match her personality, now mostly grey. Janet was fun to watch as she exercised her facial and arm animation. An observer could easily see her facial expressions migrate from disgust to exhilaration. Even today as she spoke, her waving hands threatened to slap the faces of those adjacent to her; but, being previously warned, they were watching and dodging.

President Thompson said, "Dr. Horowitz, I think you better accompany Harry and Tom to the Sanctuary to analyze our liability." Dr. Horowitz nodded.

A sudden warning, hard rapping began on the conference room door, followed immediately by the entrance of the president's Secret Service agents, who quickly stood aside to allow a delegation of armed military to enter. Leading the procession was 4 star Air Force General Warner, the previous and still current Chairman of the Joint Chief of Staff. This was one position President Dufus had not had time to replace. President Thompson appeared apprehensive, as one would under the circumstances, but stood to await the general's approach.

General Warner stood to attention, as did his team, saluted the president and said, "I represent the American Manifesto Coup. We are now in control of the military and government, and I have been sent to escort you back into the White House to resume your duties as president. Will you accept and serve again as President?"

President Thompson knew General Warner personally but returned the formal salute and said, "What about the current occupants of the White House? Won't they object? What about Congress?"

"Sir, the military has seized control of the government and arrested President Dufus and most of his family and associates, and they will be held and tried for treason. Also, since we took control of the government we are in de facto Martial Law. In other words, Congress, even without the corrupt players, is without power. If you accept our edict I am authorized by the American Manifesto to hand over the control of government to you, Sir, and we will then answer to your orders. Do you accept?"

"And what happens if I refuse?"

"Well, Sir, nothing will happen to you, but we, the military, does not want to run the government, so we will organize a new election as soon as possible. Unfortunately, however, no president will be in charge, and that poses a severe handicap to the operation of the government."

President Thompson looked around the room at the nodding heads and said, "Yes Sir. I will serve, and I'm honored to do so. I will keep my promise to Make America Great Again."

"What about my staff?"

"They are currently being, shall we say, recruited as we speak. In the interim all departments are being overseen by military personnel. The government remains at full operational standards until you replace them."

"Very well. Take me back home."

***

After the meeting Dir. Setliff said to his small group, "I need to retrieve my encrypted satellite phone provided by the Sanctuary for secure communications and call Dr. Wisscroff for transportation."

Dr. Horowitz said, "Is Dr. Wisscroff one of the Star Children?"

It was Tom Canton that laughed and said, "No. He is not a Star Child, but he is about as smart as they are, and they are brilliant. The Star Children don't use phones. They communicate among themselves via telepathy, but Dr. Wisscroff is one of the few at the Sanctuary with a satellite phone. That's who we call when we need to communicate with them."

"Actually, you will get along great with him. You are almost as old as he is. Dr. Wisscroff is over eighty years old and is a world renowned astrophysicist and Nobel Prize recipient, twice I believe. He has been a mentor and protector of the Star Children from the beginning. The Star Children sought him out at the University of Arizona when there were only six of them, and he has been with them ever since as a permanent member of the Sanctuary. He looks like a frazzled Albert Einstein and has a great deal of influence over them. He and Mr. Mum are always discussing something."

Dir. Setliff said, "Tom, save the information on Mr. Mum. Let him be a surprise."

"Right, a big surprise." Janet gave them one of her puzzled expressions and shrugged shoulders but said nothing.

Dr. Wisscroff answered on the second ring laughing and said, "Hello Dir. Setliff. We've been expecting your call. It took you long enough to figure it out."

"Yeah, we were a little slow on the uptake. Can we come meet with the team?"

After a long pause, apparently conversing with others near him, he said, "I see you are in Florida. We know where. Tom and Sue said they will be there in about an hour."

"We'll be ready."

19

A very shaken Dr. Horowitz said, "An hour? That quick? Won't we need foul weather gear for the Antarctica?"

A laughing Dir. Setliff said, "They were giving us an hour. They can be here quicker if they want. And, no we will not need foul weather gear. Just get used to surprises."

While they were waiting, Dr. Horowitz said, "I assume Tom and Sue are Star Children? By the way, just what is a Star Child?"

Dir Setliff said, "Yes they are. The Star Children were genetically engineered by an alien race, the Arcadians, to merge the DNA of the Arcadian race with Humans. Tom and Sue were among the first six that came together, and they are the oldest and de facto leaders of the Star Children. By the way, they are not even 21 years old yet." Dr. Horowitz's jaw visibly dropped and her eyes shot open in shock.

They waited on the front veranda of the resort until the call came in. It was Dr. Wisscroff notifying them to meet on the front lawn area.

Dir. Setliff said, "Janet, Tom and I have experienced this before, and we want your first experience with the Star Children unspoiled by us, so we will remain quiet to let you get the full benefit." Dr. Horowitz appeared apprehensive but curious.

As they approached the designated location they saw a shimmering, pinkish light over the lawn that flashed out, revealing a gleaming flying saucer setting on the lawn. Immediately a ramp lowered to the grass and two people, a large man and woman

20

with white hair wearing silver formfitting suits came down the ramp. The couple were both smiling and began waving and came toward them.

The large man said, "Hello Harry … Tom," shaking their hands. "It's really good to see you again. This I assume is Dr. Horowitz. I am Tom Bradley and this is Sue Chambers. We oversee the Star Children. Welcome to our world."

Tom and Sue quickly led them aboard, where Dr. Wisscroff waited. Dr. Wisscroff quickly introduced himself to Dr. Horowitz and said, "We don't want to be seen here under the current situation. That's why I'm here … to use my phone and speed up the process. We will leave immediately."

There was little to see inside, open space, translucent dome and a circular bench. Janet saw no controls, but Tom and Sue slipped head-belts on, and the saucer came to life and instantly disappeared from visual sight from outside. Janet found herself enclosed in an invisible bubble. Various colored indicators became visible on the inside of the dome, and the saucer shot up into the sky. She was still standing but felt no inertia. From the sudden take off she thought she might be thrown against the floor or bulkhead, but she felt nothing … amazing. Janet watched in awe as they streaked through the upper atmosphere into blackness. Janet looked at Dir. Setliff and Tom Canton for answers, but they just watched and smiled. They had obviously seen this all before and weren't about to spoil her experience, and Tom, Sue, and Dr. Wisscroff weren't helping either.

The speed was incredible, and she watched the Gulf of Mexico flowing below them, followed quickly by Cuba, the Caribbean Sea, Central America, and the expanding landmass of South America. Damn, this saucer was fast. They had only been flying for minutes. Wow, South America was already narrowing to a point, then it was gone. More ocean passed and they seemed to be slowing. White ice filled the viewing dome as the saucer apparently was lowering in elevation. Mile after mile of white sped under them.

Sue Chambers said, "Janet, don't be frightened. We are going underwater soon under the Ross Ice Shelf to enter the Sanctuary."

Sue's comment startled her out of a trance, and she realized that they had traveled over half-way around the world without speaking. Hell, she hadn't even bothered to sit down. Suddenly she realized what Sue had said. They were going underwater! Janet decided to sit.

Just as she saw the end of ice and open sea again, the saucer dove straight into the water and sped along just under the bottom of the thick ice shelf for miles but at a much reduced speed. The light indicators on the inside of the dome provided a digital image of the terrain for them to follow. Soon they passed into an underwater cavern in a mountain and proceed up and out of the water into a large cavern going upwards. After a few hundred feet they approached a large iris door that was opening for their passage. Soon they were parking their saucer alongside other parked saucers in what looked like a pie plate stacker. The ramp lowered and they went down and on to a stairway that led upward to another iris door. Tom and Sue stepped to the side and indicated that Janet should go through first. She nodded her understanding and stepped forward toward the door and it opened.

Janet stepped into another world, an alien world. It was bright, and white and pleasantly warm. It was a huge cavern thousands of feet wide and almost that tall with artificial light emanating from the entire curving ceiling. There were no shadows in the pristine, white city stretching out below them. It was strikingly beautiful...breathtaking, actually. From obvious experience, Tom and Sue and the others remained quiet, allowing the beauty and complexity of the Sanctuary to speak for itself. They rode through the city on a moving conveyor sidewalk, similar to an airport terminal speed walk. She saw all manner of white buildings brimmed full of material, somewhat like any American city, and each building had a sign identifying itself written in English. Janet saw a bank, cafeteria, gym, hospital, numerous supply warehouses, apartments, Archive library and others she didn't readily identify. They continued all the way through the city to an obviously external entrance where there was a grassy park just inside. In the center of the park was a raised dais surrounded by circular rows of benches. Standing on the platform was a smallish man. He was humanoid but small and alien-looking. This apparent holographic replica of an Arcadian alien stood around four feet tall, pastie complexion, large green eyes and a noticeably larger head and brain.

23

The small body looked frail, which was housed in a silver suit that apparently served as clothing and protection.

Tom said, "We bring all the new Star Children members here first thing, so they can hear about our common heritage directly from our benefactors and their forefathers. This is Mr. Mum. He is an extension of the Arcadian archive and replica of one of the last Arcadian before he passed. Mr. Mum likes to meet our visitors as well. Mr. Canton and Dir. Setliff are already acquainted with Mr. Mum." For once Dr. Horowitz was speechless, but her body language screamed with facial gestures and hand jives, much to the amusement of the others.

Tom announced, "Mr. Mum, this is Dr. Janet Horowitz. She is an attorney for President Thompson. Dr. Horowitz came with Tom Canton and Dir. Setliff."

Mr. Mum seemed to look directly at her and said. "Yes, I registered your presence and have reviewed your impressive legal record. I am pleased to meet you, and you are a welcome additional guest to our upcoming discussion. Mr. Canton and Dir. Setliff, you are always welcome here." They nodded at Mr. Mum's address.

Janet, very intelligently, said, "Awww, I - I - Ugh … thank you." She actually dipped in an animated curtsy.

"I will join you in the Arcadian Archive conference room when you are all assembled."

Tom and Sue led them toward the cafeteria for introductions, a meal, and coffee before going to the archive conference room.

Chapter 2
(Eight Months Earlier)

Tom Bradley and Sue Chambers were having lunch in the Sanctuary cafeteria when Major Burns came in. The major, now promoted to colonel by President Thompson for his efforts fighting with the Star Children during the Alien War, saw them and came directly toward them. From experience they saw the stress on his face and knew something serious was about to befall them. Colonel Burns and his detachment of Marines had been their defenders since the beginning and was now a permanent attachment to the Sanctuary and the Star Children. Even if the new president reassigned him, they knew he would not go. He and his men had earned their membership here and belonged. The Star Children had retrieved the colonel's wife and they liked it here. Colonel Burns remained standing and waited to be acknowledge.

Tom said, "Good morning, colonel. You look serious. What's up?"

"Sir," Tom had never been successful in getting the colonel to call him Tom, "There is a delegation of fifteen generals and admirals at the outside gate wanting entrance to meet with representatives of the Star Children. They flew in on a private military plane. They landed in a blizzard and ask our outside guards to bring them down through the shaft through the ice shelf the Star Children opened initially. They are waiting on the outside for permission to enter. As the leaders, I'm bringing you their request."

Tom looked at Sue, who just shrugged, then asked, "Do you have any idea what they want? Do you trust them?"

"I have a feeling that I know what they want, but I would prefer to let them present their own case. It's strange that they come in secret, but I know most of them, and I do trust them. These are the good guys. If you will see them I will have them escorted by my Marines."

"Very well. Bring them to the conference room at the archive. We will bring Dr. Wisscroff and Mrs. Wilks with us to hear their presentation and requests. We value their experience and wisdom. I will also invite Mr. Mum to transfer his presence and join us in the conference room. This sounds serious."

Any of the 40 Star Children would be welcome, but Tom and Sue, on impulse, specifically invited Berta, along with the targeted humans. They had gathered in the archive conference room and were waiting when the delegation entered. Tom had seen many high ranking military during the Alien Wars and his brief time around President Thompson, but he couldn't remember ever seeing so much gold braid and flashy medals as was on display today. Apparently the delegation came in full formal dress, and the lowest rank among them was three stars. This group wanted to make an impression, and indeed they did. The large room was now full of borrowed chairs to accommodate the extra fifteen high ranking officers. Even so, Colonel Burns stood, along with his squad of combat Marines, behind the delegation. Tom knew that Colonel Burns was loyal to the Star Children and any of these ranking officers would not change that.

Tom Bradly said, "Welcome to the Sanctuary." He didn't wait for a response. "You have obviously gone to great deal of effort to come to us secretly. Well, you have our attention. Please let us know what you desire from us."

A tall, lean and straight general with a chest full of medals stood to attention and said, "Mr. Bradley, I am Air Force General Ron Warner. You may remember me as the Chairman of the Joint Chief of Staff under President Thompson." Tom did remember him as a friend. He had been the commanding general during the Alien War. "I represent a movement of 130 + admirals and generals from all branches of service, and I and this group hope to solicit the help of the Star Children to help us with a military Coup of the United States." He paused long enough for that information to settle. "A Coup is the only conceivable way to prevent an all-out armed revolution of its citizens. The citizens of the U.S. are consolidating, organizing, and arming themselves. It is unstoppable at this point. The military will be charged with the defense of the nation to fight our own citizens. Millions of innocent people will die in an open revolt, and in the process, the United States will become extremely vulnerable from Russia and China and even terrorist attacks when this happens. You already know about the fleets of attack saucers the U.S. and Russia already have, and we suspect

China has them as well. You stopped them before, and quite frankly, the Star Children are the only ones that can stop them again if they are deployed. We want you to help us with this Coup and defend us against any saucer attacks. This is why we are here. We need help."

Sue Chambers said, "Why should we get involved? We have no stake in a revolution or war with other nations for that matter."

The general said, "Because you care about humanity, and without your help the world could explode into anarchy and chaos. The Star Children prevented the world domination by the NAZIs from the Underworld, and you control them still. Without your help the globalist and Communist will take over the United States and they will accomplish what the NAZIs tried to do."

Sue said, "What you say about the NAZIs is true, but they were trying to kill us off and almost did. We defended ourselves and helped you in the process. We also helped the Russians."

The indignant general said, "If the Communist/Globalist succeed in taking over the United States and forming a one world Communist (globalist) government, how long do you think it will take before they come after you? At that point they will be unbelievably powerful and focused. The Star Children remain a threat to their agenda, and threats to them must be eliminated at all cost. Don't you think saving America will ensure you have a strong ally in that potential future battle?

Tom said, "Dr. Wisscroff, what are your thoughts?"

28

The grizzled and wooly scholar thought in silence before speaking, "I think there is a lot of sense in what the general is saying, but we must give this much thought and deep discussions and planning. I would suggest that you bring in your doppelgänger, John Meeker, from his management of the Underworld. As I recall, he was educated in political science and served as an assistant to the Brazilian Ambassador before he was identified as a Star Child. He may be able to provide additional insight to this discussion. His Star Child mate, Jane Turret, as I also remember, served as interpreter to the Russian president. I believe she might be able to address the potential Russian involvement."

"I see you have brought Berta to this meeting. You must have anticipated this potential discussion. I agree and think we might need her technical savvy, certainly in our initial discussion."

"Thank you, Dr. Wisscroff for your comments. They are appreciated as always. I will contact John and Janet to solicit their input. Mrs. Wilks, do you have any comments so far?"

Mrs. Wilks, the mother hen of the Star Children and conscience of them all, said, "Hummm, I have dealt with bullies all my life and teaching career, and I see the makings of a super-bully in the form of a one-world government of a few powerful leaders. Freedom is at stake, and this scares me. I think we need to talk more."

Tom said, "Thank you. Mr. Mum, I saved you for last. Do you have an opinion?"

Mr. Mum's holographic image flashed to life over the conference table, startling all, especially

29

the delegation, having never met or even heard about him. Mr. Mum said, "Arcadians are not noted for their clever subterfuge. We are inherently always focused toward helping humanity, not manipulating or dominating it. The archive can provide little useful help toward this goal. I will say, however, I tend to agree with the future concerns presented. Further discussion may be warranted."

Tom said, "Well, General Warner, it looks like you have got our attention. We will discuss this further. We invite you to stay with us while we decide if and how we can help."

The general looked relieved and visibly relaxed his previously rigid shoulders slightly. The general said, "Thank you, Mr. Bradly and team. We welcome staying here while we talk."

Tom continued, "Please see Mrs. Wilks after we break up, and she will assign you living quarters, then join us for lunch in the cafeteria. I will contact John Meeker and ask him and Jane Turret to join us."

Tom telepathically sent a message to John and Jane giving them a brief explanation of the meeting and invitation to join in, without going into detail. They both actually jumped at the chance to return to the Sanctuary. Since John had become Supreme Commander of the NAZIs and the Underworld, they had been somewhat isolated. Apparently both were lonesome for Star Children interface.

John had taken one of the Arcadian saucers for self-defense and transportation, since only an Arcadian saucer could enter the Sanctuary through the underground cave security. They both had a premonition of what this was about and left immediately, bringing what would be a surprise and unexpected guest.

After being assigned quarters, being introduced around, and having lunch; the military delegation returned to the conference room wearing less formal attire. Their medals had been replaced with only the battle ribbons, still quite impressive decoration on their chests. Once they were again seated, John, Jane, and a tall, rigidly straight, white-haired gentleman dressed in full NAZI military regalia entered. The uniform was black with an Iron Cross around his neck and four gleaming stars, complete with the SS insignia and red swastika arm band on his left sleeve. The reaction was immediate.

General Warner and many of the others of the delegation jumped to their feet and General Warner bellowed, "What is the meaning of this obvious insult to us?" The uniformed NAZI remained calm and standing rigid.

Tom Bradley said, "Calm yourselves. I wasn't expecting this guest, but I can assure you that no insult was or is intended. Let me introduce John Meeker and Jane Turret. They can explain and introduce their guest."

The three stood at the podium and John Meeker spoke. "I am John Meeker and my new wife, Jane." Congratulations were voiced. "I am the Supreme Commander of the NAZIs and the Underworld, including the alien race of Resis, also making the Underworld home. My guest is active General Max Bruner of the Schutzstaffel (SS), and he is the commander of the Underground's military.

Absolutely no disrespect is intended by the general's attire. This is his normal attire in the Underworld. I brought General Bruner here today because we strongly suspected the reason for your delegation, and if we are correct in our assumption, General Bruner can provide valuable advice from his long experience, which would support your goal." The delegation then reluctantly calmed and took their seats.

The delegation remained in shock but visibly relaxed and General Warner said, "We apologize for our reaction. We thought we were becoming the butt of a joke. We were just shocked at seeing a German SS general in uniform decades after our World War II ended. How is this possible?"

John said, "The NAZI military base here in the Underworld never surrendered and didn't recognized Germany's surrender. The NAZI leadership relocated to Antarctica and remained sequestered and continued their war in secret. Their army and plans for a 4th Reich were defeated in the Alien War, but their society remains intact. I became the new Supreme Commander by mortal combat, you may remember the contest transmitted worldwide at the time. As their leader, I keep them sequestered; but I couldn't alter their society overnight, nor can we allow them to migrate from the Underworld. So we live peacefully with the world in our own home in the Underworld. I hope this answers your questions and concerns."

General Warner and the others of the delegation, out of new, hesitant respect, saluted General Bruner, which was returned. General

Warner then said, "I believe this group probably has guessed the reason for our visit. Yes, we contemplate a military coup, and we seek the advice and assistance of the Star Children."

John Meeker said, "Thank you for formally clarifying your intent. This is why I brought General Bruner. The general led the planning for world domination of the 4th Reich prior to and during the Alien War, which came within a breath of succeeding. He understands the planning required for a Coup of this magnitude far beyond any others and is here to offer advice and help. I will let him speak, but he first wants to make sure you know what you are getting into and the complexities."

General Bruner stood at the podium and said, "Before I address you, I'm sure you may have questions. I think we should get those out of the way so we can concentrate on the subject at hand … a military Coup."

Admiral Jones asked, "Why would you agree to help us?"

General Bruner actually laughed, then said, "I have several reasons, but mainly I like the challenge. You are probably unaware that many of our race, the new master NAZI race, are genetically altered. We actually stole some DNA fragments from the Arcadians and have some of their traits and powers, however, we maintained our own identity. We are of a far higher intellect than normal humans, but we maintained our aggressiveness and manipulative dominance, unlike the benevolent Star Children. I guess you could say we are malevolent, while they are benevolent. John Meeker says this

33

makes us psychopaths without empathy or remorse and gives us an arrogant and annoying personality among normal humans, but we don't really care." This revelation brought chuckles from the delegation and others around the table.

"Another reason is that, since our failed world Coup, we are now vulnerable to destruction. Previously we had limited control over the world governments and armies through our decades long deployment of the explosive implants we used to control them, but once they were discovered by the Star Children and removed, the Communists were free to resume their global conquest. If America falls under the control of the Communist, they will quickly achieve world dominance."

"Once the Communist achieve world control we, the Underworld and Sanctuary, will become their targets. We were relatively safe from a nuclear attack before, which is the only weapon capable of destroying us, because the citizens had a voice in American government, which was mirrored in other world government and allies. We observed that with the theft of the last corrupt election, this voice is now gone, and the citizens no longer have any control over their government. With a consolidated global Communist government ruled by a few wealthy and powerful individuals, it would not be a major concern to the elite if millions of people drown around the world from the sudden melting of the southern ice cap from a nuclear detonation. From their point of view that might even seem desirable, fewer people to have to deal with."

"Look at what the Communist did to steal the American election. Anyone with a brain knows that China released the COVID virus to spread around the world. They killed millions just to influence and take control of the American election through their controlled absentee ballots procedures. They had planned that move for years, and it was a brilliant plan that worked."

Dr. Wisscroff interrupted and said, "Do you have evidence to prove they released the virus intentionally? That's an incredible claim. Would any government, Communist or not, actually kill millions of humans just to win an election?"

"Damn, Dr. Wisscroff, you sound like one of them! That's one of their canned responses they offer. The answer to your question, however, is of course they would and did. There is a plethora of evidence to prove that fact, but your government, media, DOJ, FBI … hell all of them, ignore the evidence; and the average citizen is a victim of the controlled media narrative. Ask Berta if it's true after she begins her IT research. John tells me Berta is incredible with technology, and if she is, she will find it quickly. But, I already know, because it is something I would have done."

"I'll give one better to consider. We in the Underworld strongly suspect they will do it again to steal the next election. The Underworld doesn't have the advanced technology to retrieve the information we seek to prove it, but we strongly suspect a weaponized version of the Smallpox virus will be released in time to lock down and steal the next election as well. After that there will be no more elections. Yes, they will kill far more with their next wave, but they will complete their takeover of America, then the world. If they can kill millions by releasing a virus, there is no doubt they won't hesitate to kill millions more by nuking us here."

"Keep in mind also, China is severely overpopulated, along with most of the rest of the world. Earth has more people than it can feed and support. They seek to reduce the world population, and a virus would do just that."

"Think about it. The Communist now control, the House, Senate, and Presidency. They will do anything … Anything … to maintain and strengthen that strangle hold on America. When they achieve their goal, they will come after us here. They will want to solidify their control by eliminating the last resistance to their power by destroying the Sanctuary and the Underworld. It will happen as soon as they complete the takeover of America and consolidate. This is the Underworld's motivation and reasoning."

A Marine 3-Star General Toma asked, "If you are so concerned why haven't you already started to fight back?"

"I have been trying to convince John Meeker of this for a while, but he is not yet convinced. The Underworld is not a democracy or a republic, John is our Supreme Commander, and he has absolute authority over us. Additionally, it is also beyond our abilities alone at this late point. The Underworld has lost its power, influence, our Resis alien workers and fighters, and any advantage we once had. And, the Sanctuary is extremely powerful but too small. Even together we cannot fight the world, even if the Star Children were so inclined. This is why I'm personally pleased to see you gentlemen and lady seek their help. It gives me the opportunity to present my case to the Star Children."

Dr. Wisscroff said, "General Warner, maybe you should tell us why you want a Coup before we discuss this further. What are your motivations?"

General Warner took a deep breath and said, "I … we", spreading his arms to include the delegation, "We want to save the United States of America. We have got to get this idiot, Communist president out before he can completely destroys America. One major example is Afghanistan. We totally won the war in Afghanistan, but this idiot pulled us out and let the terrorist enemy walk right back in and take it over, again. Even worst, he pulled the military out so fast and made us leave all of our weapons and equipment there. We left over 85 billion dollars in weapons and equipment. That is billions with a capital 'B'. Can you believe the insanity? He wouldn't even let us bring our equipment back. I mean we won the damn war there and he gave it back and armed them with our own weapons. We left helicopters, vehicles, all kind of advanced weapons, and equipped and stocked bases they moved right into. Now they have high tech weapons to use against us … against *us* and their neighboring countries. When they come against us again in the region, and they will, we will lose soldiers killed by our own weapons taking back a

37

country we had already defeated. This president is a disaster, and we must take him out of office."

"America was energy independent for the first time in decades when President Thompson was in office, and we were even exporting gas. The price of gas at the pump was under $2.00 p/gal. The first thing President Dufus did was close down the Keystone Pipeline and cripple our oil industry. Now the price of gas is over $7.00 p/gal., and the price per barrel is the highest it's ever been, which we are having to purchase. The outpouring of funds to hostile countries is staggering. We are transferring out our wealth, and driving America into bankruptcy."

"He is quickly eliminating excellent, high ranking, knowledgeable officers and replacing them with Marxist operators. He doesn't want an armed forces to defend America, he wants to neutralize, weaken and neuter our military so we can't defend ourselves."

"He opened our secure borders wide for illegal immigrants, and we have no control or idea who is coming in. Potential terrorist and combatants are coming into the US in droves. Additionally, they are not being screened at all for diseases."

"He and his administration are spending money like a drunken sailor, sorry admirals for that reference. We are being reduced to a bankrupt country with no defense, which is part of the socialist plan. If we don't move fast he will succeed."

General Toma said, "General Bruner, I'm trying to catch up. Can we go back a ways and help bring some of us up to speed? I'm not sure what you mean by Resis, alien fighters, and exactly what is the Underworld?"

General Bruner smiled and said, "The answers are simple but have been hidden from the world. Hopefully we are now on the same side, but if we lose this battle you're here to discuss, it will not matter, so I will reveal them. The Underground is what it sounds like. It is a huge underground cavern deep below the ice cap almost as large as some continents. The entrance is hidden and will remain so. Hitler's explorers and scientists discovered it before WW-II, and the NAZI Reich moved into it even before we began losing the war. We intended to rule the 4th Reich and the world from there, and we almost did."

"The Resis is a race of ancient aliens we discovered living in the Underworld that possessed abandoned and lost advanced technology we acquired and improved upon. The Resis were under our control and became our flying saucer pilots and infantry we were going to use in our attack on the world. As you know, the Star Children foiled those plans and we retreated back to the Underworld. John Meeker challenged our Supreme Commander to combat and defeated him, making him the new Supreme Commander. He released the Resis from our control, and we now share the Underworld as co-inhabitants."

General Warner injected, "For those in the delegation not familiar with what happened during the Alien War, the NAZI scientist discovered anti-gravity technology when they entered the

39

Underworld and developed it for use into flying saucers. They controlled and trained the Resis to fly them, and due to unexpected crashes, Russia and America got the technology and secretly developed fleets of saucers. For us it was the launch of our secret base at Area 51. The Alien War was all about the Resis taking over those fleets and attacking the world. Fortunately for the world, the Star Children's saucers were better. The war came down to Star Children versus Resis, thus it was called the Alien War. I hope this helps."

General Bruner continued, "I truly understand your plight and your desire for a Coup, but my only concern is how committed you are, and if you are willing to do what is necessary. A partial Coup will not solve your problem. You must go all the way." The last statement was an obvious challenge.

It was Dr. Wisscroff that responded to the challenge and asked, "What are you suggesting that we do?"

General Bruner smiled and said, "You must be willing to do a complete and all-encompassing Coup of most, if not all, of the high level corrupted Communist elite in America, and this will take the assassination of possibly millions. In addition you must take their funds." The general then sat down and let the wailing begin.

The table was abuzz with cries of outrage, indignation, unbelievable aggravation at the very suggestion that assassinations be used in a Coup. It took many long moments before the chorus of voices settled to a level where anyone could voice a focused comment.

40

Tom Bradley finally said, "You can't be serious. John is he serious?"

John said, "I'm afraid he is very serious, and he has convince me, even Jane, that he is correct. When you are ready to listen, the general can present his reasoning and strategy. It makes sense. I think you should reserve your judgment until he is finished."

General Warner said, "That was a shocker, but I'm curious enough to listen." Others nodded in agreement, but Sue Chambers' face remained screwed up in disgust.

General Bruner stood again at the podium and said, "I hesitate to try and tell you that you have absolutely no idea who you are up against and how powerful, wealthy, and entrenched they are, but unfortunately you don't. The Communist ideology has been in play in America even before WW II. It took the Japanese bombing of Pearl Harbor before America entered the war, which most reasonable people knew was inevitable. You are just lucky the British and Russians held on as long as they did, or you would have been alone and lost the war. The Communist have entrenched themselves in every facet of life in America. Your recent President Odumby managed to complete the corruption of all facets of your government with Communist operatives, they call themselves progressive. He successfully managed to corrupt and weaponize the IRS, DOJ, FBI, CIA, and many other government agencies to support the progressive (Communist) agenda, and with the last corrupted election, they have effectively completed their takeover and ensured there will never be another non-Communist ever elected. They now have a Communist president and administration plus control of the House and Senate. If that remains, they will attack and eliminate all patriots from government then start on the citizens."

"If you think you can defeat them in the political arena you are sadly mistaken. Your President Thompson tried too, as he called it, 'Drain the Swamp', and failed. The swamp rose up and drown him with corruption. The entrenched Communist in politics, corporate management, unions, and the media fought and crucified him at every turn and succeeded in finally expelling him by fake news, lies, deceit, and corruption. No, if anyone could have done it, it was President Thompson. The corruption must be eliminated by mass assassinations. You have to cut the cancer out or it will destroy the entire body."

Sue said, "You have used several names: Communist, Marxist, socialist, progressive, liberals, and corrupted to describe the enemy. Are you putting them all together in one category? What is the difference?"

"If you are asking me what is the difference between democracy and Communism, the basic difference is that democracy has checks and balances and Communism has none. The Communist elite control everything. Unfortunately, all those checks and balances in America now no longer exist once all the agencies have been weaponized."

42

"If you are asking me the differences between all those titles, for the most part they are all the product of Marxist ideology. There are, however, several categories of Communist. You have the card carrying and dedicated and hard-lined Communist. They have a defined agenda and continually strive to achieve their goals. You have Communist that are a product of a corrupted, public education and decades of ideology indoctrination. They blindly believe what they are told by the corrupted mainstream media and support and vote according to the elite Communist leadership and instructions. Then you have the duped and uninformed Communist. This group is typically uneducated, apathetic, and easily influenced and tend to follow. They don't even know they are Communist and just follow along with the Marxist agenda as they have been taught. Socialist, progressive, and liberals are synonymous with Communist. They basically mean the same thing. You also mentioned corrupted. I use this word to mean that they have another agenda other than working for the best interest of the country. They have a corrupted agenda to gain personal wealth and power at the expense of the nation, which fits well into the Communist goals. I hope this helps."

Sue said, "Yes, I have a better understanding of where you are coming from. But, still, assassinations is a horrible concept to employ. I can't believe we could resort to killing off our opposition. That's a terrible example to set or start."

General Bruner said, "Miss Chambers, with all due respect, you were raised in America and

Americans are spoiled to your own ideas of what life should be like and not what is reality in most of the world. For the most part you have never experienced hunger, I mean real life-threatening and painful hunger. You have not been exposed to real abuse where your parents and loved ones are shot and killed in front of you because they don't agree with the Communist leadership. You have always been free and have never been forced to live under Communist or dictator rule, like America will soon experience if it's not stopped. Many of your immigrants understand it only too well, because they came to America for the freedom most Americans take for granted. They came to escape Communism, something you admittedly don't truly understand. In short, Miss Chambers, Americans are incredibly naive, and you are a classic example."

"You show your naivety to suggest we would be starting something new when assassinations in political coups are common place, even necessary. People that disagree or threaten the ruling or intended ruling authority must be and are always eliminated in one form or another. They must be silenced or eliminated for it to work. Our discussed Coup is a conservative political Coup, and if it is to succeed we must do the same thing. The only difference in this Coup is the nature of the ruler. In General Warner's discussed case for America means Freedom ruled by the people according to the Constitution of the United States through its elected representatives of the people as opposed to a Communist ruled America where you have no choice. But, a government ruled by the Constitution must also maintain that rule by eliminating its threats, something America has failed to do internally. Again, you are naive to think that America hasn't and doesn't do assassinations to maintain its rule. America has armies to do that, and almost every government agency has strike teams to eliminate threats of all kinds, foreign and domestic. Most are kept secret of course, but people die in accidents, unanticipated heart attacks, and other natural causes all the time. Don't kid yourself. People die all the time. You just don't hear about it in the controlled news."

"America's problem is that they haven't exercised that option enough and allowed corrupted operatives to gain access and work toward their agenda from within and they now control them. Now if you want your Constitution to rule over America, you need to clean out the chaff once and for all. If not, Communism will take control. There are only the two options, and that is what needs to be decided here." Sue listen intently without comment and didn't become angered. Maybe she asked the question to force the discussion.

Dr. Wisscroff said, "I'm listening intently to the discussion through aged ears. When I say aged I mean I have lived a long time and have seen many world events through these eyes. I must agree with General Bruner. Americans are spoiled and naive. We see the world through the biased nightly news, and we see what we are allowed to see, but we have no idea what is really happening. Americans live in a controlled capsule."

"I'm an astrophysics and never considered myself a philosopher, but much the general is saying is true. It is human nature to group together for the common defense, food production, etc. In any group they must come together with common goals, and when that doesn't happen controversy arises. When controversy happens the larger or stronger segment tends to rule and control the rest. As individual groups grow they get stronger. I remember the fascist growth and expansion in Europe. That intolerant group expanded and began to dominate countries and even launched a massive extermination of an entire race of people. World War II began to resist these fascist. Europe had only two choices: Let the fascist take over and continue their expansion or fight back. They fought back and 75,000,000 humans died in that conflict."

"We find ourselves in a similar dilemma today with Communism, and again we have only two choices: Let them win and take over or fight back. I'm inclined to fight back, but unique in this situation, the casualties would probably be under a million with an assassination Coup as opposed to many millions in an open rebellion. The choice seems clear, protect our Constitution and way of life."

Mrs. Wilks said, "As many of you know I've been a teacher most of my life, and among the subjects I taught was history. If history teaches us anything, dominance and power leads to war. This is human nature. History is full of wars and death dating back as far as history is recorded. Just read about Hannibal, Napoleon, Attila the Hun,

Alexander the Great, Julius Caesar, and Hitler, among many others. All of them attempted to rule the known world. Some even succeeded. Nothing has changed. This is what we are facing again. Yes, history tells us war is coming. It's inevitable. General Bruner tells us that there are only two options, capitulate or fight back. I for one don't believe in capitulating to corrupt leaders, but I'm beginning to see a third option in the way we fight back."

General Bruner said, "That's well said, both of you. Thank you. I think we are coming together. Now, concerning a potential Hit List for my proposed Coup, it already exists. Fortunately, the Underworld has been tracking them for decades for our own purposes, and we know who they are and all their deeds. We also know those on the side of democracy, because they were on *our* hit list. They would have resisted a takeover of the 4th Reich. For our proposed Hit List for a potential Coup we just have to switch them around."

"An armed revolution will not solve your problem, because the Communist will still be entrenched in government and the media. You will still need them gone … eliminated. Unless you do that, a military Coup will not work. They will still be in place to isolate and prosecute you one by one. Another thing to consider are the casualties of a violent conflict. Millions will die, and the deaths will not be among the ranking Communist. Those dead will mostly be the patriots. No, the deaths need to be among the anarchist. Let the Communist offenders die as opposed to the citizens you are

47

attempting to save. Remember your civil war. The plantation owners and elite didn't die. It was the young warriors sent out to fight."

"Think about it sensibly, and you will see that I'm right. So you will better understand what you are up against and the level of the opposition, let me provide you with some additional history of America. The changes have been subtle and occurred over decades and generations, and most citizens don't even realize the changes that have been implemented. Many of those here are too young to have even seen the changes. To you it's the way it has always been, just worse."

"In the early '60's during the days of the 'former' Soviet Union, Russian Premier Nikita Khrushchev pounded his shoe on the podium of the United Nations and shouted to the West, 'We will bury you!' Fearing an invasion from the Reds, America proceeded to build the most awesome military machine in history. Unfortunately, America forgot to guard its political home front from being taken over by socialist - Communist - liberal activists who would gain office and destroy American law by a process of gradually installing the Communist agenda within your legal system and separate branches of government."

"They are a large worldwide organization, heavily funded, well organized, with dedicated long-term goals and a commitment to a one world government. "They are the Communist Party, and 'They' have already won! "They have an agenda that they have religiously followed that has mostly been accomplished over decades . They don't even care that you know their goals, since "They" already achieved most of them."

"If you doubt me for saying they have succeeded, I encourage you to read the 45 goals of the Communist Party established in print and recorded in the Congressional record in 1963. Many are complicated and require research to validate the goals already achieved, but many are simply stated and easy to verify or are self-explanatory." The general handed a stack of papers to the nearest person to be passed around. "Please read their published *Communist Manifesto* of 45 goals. I and my staff have researched most of them and provided our response. The list is sobering. Our report is short, but if you would like a second opinion or greater details, I suggest you read, *The Naked Communist*, by Dr. Rich Swier. In his book he provided far more details and researched facts, but we weren't all that interested at that time. I believe the short list will make my point."

Communist Manifesto

#1. U.S. acceptance of coexistence as the only alternative to atomic war.

The Treaty on the Nonproliferation of Nuclear Weapons, known as the Non-Proliferation Treaty or NPT originally accomplished this goal. Five states are recognized by NPT as nuclear weapon states (NWS): China (signed 1992), France (1992), the Soviet Union (1968 and subsequently the Russian Federation after the collapse of the Soviet Union), the United Kingdom (1968), and the United States (1968). These five nations are also the five permanent members of the United Nations Security Council.

The UN treaty became official in 1970. Its declared objective was to prevent the spread of nuclear weapons and weapons technology, to promote cooperation and share nuclear technology for peaceful uses, and to further the goal of achieving nuclear disarmament.

This NPT treaty drastically hampered the U.S.'s development of nuclear technology, which it was designed to do. Since its original launch "They" have continued to use the NPT to reduce our nuclear deployment arsenal and our defense through many additional treaties. President Obama pushed this agenda forward at an even faster pace with the New START treaty ratified in 2011. The language of the treaty reduced America's nuclear weapon capacity but didn't reduce Russia's, and Russia would maintained a 10–1 advantage in tactical nuclear weapons, which were not counted in the treaty. Agreeing to the new treaty put America in an unfair disadvantage, which it was intended to do.

#2. U.S. willingness to capitulate in preference to engaging in atomic war.

This premise has been increasingly encouraged as the internal corruption grows. We have only to look at Obama's capitulation to Russia on the missile defense system for Poland and parts of Europe, the New Start treaty, Iran nuclear deal,

Cooperative Threat Reduction Program. It can be seen in the stiff liberal opposition to any attempt to strengthen the U.S. position. The obvious attempt is to weaken and bankrupt the U.S.

#3. Develop the illusion that total disarmament [by] the United States would be a demonstration of moral strength.

How often have we heard this crap? Does any sane person believe this? If the U.S. totally disarmed it would not show moral strength, it would be a total capitulation. This would be the same as waving a white flag and surrendering. This is, of course, what "They" want. Can you imagine a world with nuclear weapons and the U.S. with none?

We can also include gun control within this category. "They" do not want guns maintained by citizens and will use any argument to push gun control and disarmament of the citizen. The result would be the same. Let's not forget that the Second Amendment was a guarantee to the citizens to have the ability to fight back against a tyrannical government.

#4. Permit free trade between all nations regardless of Communist affiliation and regardless of whether or not items could be used for war.

There have been many free trade agreements for the U.S., with the biggest being the North

American Free Trade Agreement (NAFTA) signed in 1994. This free trade agreement had the effect of eliminating import tax from Canada and Mexico. This began an ever increasing trade deficit to the U.S., massive transfer of our wealth, and started a mass defection of our U.S. companies to Mexico. It didn't take a rocket scientist to figure this result out. "They" figured that the average citizen wouldn't understand this, but decades later we have learned, as the U.S. approaches bankruptcy. The Trans Pacific Partnership (TPP) pushed by President Obama would have been even worse. "They" have almost succeeded in taking our wealth, companies, and jobs.

#5. Extension of long-term loans to Russia and Soviet satellites.

This is blatantly obvious.

#6. Provide American aid to all nations regardless of Communist domination.

Of course "They" want American aid given to Communist countries, but why would we want that? It is so incredibly obvious of their goals to promote Communism and deplete America's wealth. Why can't the people see this? Many are simply uninformed, plus the push has developed slowly over a long period of time, and if you don't know who "They" are and their goals it's hard to see it coming. Many, before they learn, think surely "They" know what they are doing. Well, "They" do know what they are doing and what their goals are, but their goals are different, unless you are one of the "They".

#7. Grant recognition of Red China. Admission of Red China to the U.N.

This was accomplished in 1971 by officially replacing the Republic of China with the Peoples Republic of China (Communist Red China). Not only did this bring Red China into the U.N., but Red China replaced the original Republic of China as one of the five Permanent Security Council members with veto powers of the U.N.

#8. Set up East and West Germany as separate states in spite of Khrushchev's promise in 1955 to settle the German question by free elections under supervision of the U.N.

#9. Prolong the conferences to ban atomic tests because the United States has agreed to suspend tests as long as negotiations are in progress.

#10. Allow all Soviet satellites individual representation in the U.N.

The obvious goal here is to take over the U.N. and turn it Communist.

#11. Promote the U.N. as the only hope for mankind. If its charter is rewritten, demand that

it be set up as a one-world government with its own independent armed forces.

The "They" launched a two-prong political attack against the U. S., a destruction and take over from the inside and an outside attack from the United Nations, which "They" have managed to significantly infiltrate and control. Openly, the U.N. wants and promotes a one-world government controlled by them, a Communist government.

#12. Resist any attempt to outlaw the Communist Party.

#13. Do away with all loyalty oaths.

#14. Continue giving Russia access to the U.S. Patent Office.

#15. Capture one or both of the political parties in the United States.

"They" have abandoned the name Communist. That name has too many negative connotations. "They" go by many names today like Liberal and Socialist but mostly "Progressive" is used, and the Democrat Party is now considered the Progressive (Communist) Party. The #15 goal is to capture both the Democrat and Republican parties. They have completely succeeded with the Democrat Party and President Obama moved the goals agenda decidedly forward during his administration. It is sad indeed to see the Democratic Party, once a party of the people, now dominated by the far left, radicals of the party. The Republican Party has far too many RINOs (Republican In Name Only) and have done their share of damage to America as well. Luckily, the Republican Party still has some true Americans patriates remaining, but they are fading.

#16. Use technical decisions of the courts to weaken basic American institutions by claiming their activities violate civil rights.

Control of the Supreme Court has long been the objective. "They" want the Supreme Court to be predominantly Liberal (Communist), and they have almost reached that goal as evidenced by the fact that most controversial decision are decided by 5 - 4 votes. The current president makes the decision of the nomination; although the nominee must be confirmed by the Senate, which is becoming increasingly divided and partisan. One such Supreme Court vote and classic example was the Defense of Marriage Act. Most states already had or were in the process of legislating their laws to define marriage as one male and one female. Many of these states had it in their constitutions. "They" obviously couldn't get what they wanted by the vote of the people and used the law to enforce their view upon everyone. Handpicked federal judges had been successful in ruling many of the state laws as unconstitutional, and President Clinton pushed Defense of Marriage Act (DOMA) to bring it under federal law. The only way "They" could stop and reverse DOMA was to have it declared unconstitutional, which was done by the Supreme Court in 2013 with a 5 - 4 vote.

"They" have spent decades trying to take control of the Supreme Court with Liberal judges and gained a large step forward when President Clinton nominated Ruth Bader Ginsburg to the Supreme Court in 1991. Justice Ginsburg was previously an activist liberal attorney for the ACLU, a far left organization. Further advancements of the liberal goals came with the addition of Justice Sonia Sotomayor in 2009 and Justice Elena Kagan in 2010, both nominated by President Obama. The shift to near domination by liberal Justices was almost complete.

#17. Get control of the schools. Use them as transmission belts for socialism and current Communist propaganda. Soften the curriculum. Get control of teachers' associations. Put the party line in textbooks.

This goal has been one of the most devastating accomplishment and crowning victory for Communism, which was launched against our children. What's sad is that we let it happen. "They" have invested many years and generation toward this goal accomplishment, which started long before these 45 goals were documented. Teach the young, and they will grow up socialist. Do it slowly over many years and they will not even know they have been indoctrinated ... they will simply be. They become the "They" of tomorrow.

The intent (goal) is to get control of what the children, through college, learn by changing the textbooks to control the curriculum. Become the teachers and infiltrate the teachers associations. "They" have succeeded.

"They" have slowly consolidated the power of teachers' associations into federal organizations to gain control over the states. In 1979 President Johnson pushed the first federal program, National Education Association (NEA), and in 1980 the very progressive President Carter took office and pushed, created and signed into law the federal Department of Education. This law and department enforced federal education laws and civil rights over all states, (see #16). The Republicans tried to repeal and reverse this law, but both Bush presidents moved in lock-steps to keep in going, even advancing it. In the beginning it did some good, but once the control tentacles were established it has been used for the total control (goal obtained) over education and implementation of the many social programs forced upon the states.

The National Education Association (NEA) today is the largest union in the U.S.. The American Federation of Teachers (AFT) is the second largest (see #36). These unions have a massive political lobby and influence over the education of our youth, and "They" are predominantly progressive socialist. To insure their control "They" want total control over children's education and fight any attempts to provide voucher or charter school options, eliminate tenure (ability to fire) or regulations.

57

#18. Gain control of all student newspapers.

#19. Use student riots to foment public protests against programs or organizations which are under Communist attack.

#20 Infiltrate the press. Get control of book-review assignments, editorial writing, policymaking positions.)

It is easy to see that the press can find no fault with the Democrats and can find no good with the Republicans (conservative) unless they happen to agree with them and their agenda. This only works if the Democrats and the Press and others are following the same agenda, which they obviously are. Lies are told and the press generates fake news to support the lies. Any genuine Republican (Conservative) must campaign against their Democrat opponent AND the Press. Under this category we also find many of the pollsters that seem to always stretch the Democrat candidates true poles and denigrate their opponent.

#21 Gain control of key positions in radio, TV, and motion pictures.

This goes right along with #20. Think about the what are called "Talking Heads" or political analysts that try to tell the viewers what and how to think. "They" put their liberal spin on the news, which always seems to be in alliance with their listed goals. Those that keep themselves better

58

informed than most, can recognize the lies and subtle twists of their diatribe. What is unbelievable is just how many uninformed people tend to believe them.

#22. Continue discrediting American culture by degrading all forms of artistic expression.

An American Communist cell was told to "eliminate all good sculpture from parks and buildings, substitute shapeless, awkward and meaningless forms."

#23. Control art critics and directors of art museums.

"Our plan is to promote ugliness, repulsive, meaningless art."

#24. Eliminate all laws governing obscenity by calling them "censorship" and a violation of free speech and free press.

#25. Break down cultural standards of morality by promoting pornography and obscenity in books, magazines, motion pictures, radio, and TV.

Does anyone doubt this goal has been obtained?

#26. Present homosexuality, degeneracy and promiscuity as "normal, natural, healthy."

#27. Infiltrate the churches and replace revealed religion with "social" religion. Discredit the Bible and emphasize the need for intellectual maturity, which does not need a "religious crutch."

This goal led to "social religion" such as Atheism, Humanism, Scientology, a now recognized religion created by a Science Fiction writer. There are others such as black nationalist such as Rev. Jeremiah Wright, Louis Farrakhan, Al Sharpton, Jessie Jackson. Many of these preach racists hate and anti-American treason. In 1954 while the tax codes were being written for 501C tax exempt organizations, Senator Johnson added an amendment, now called the Johnson Amendment, preventing churches from becoming political. This amendment has totally silenced churches. For years this amendment has been selectively used to keep churches muzzled. In 2010 through 2012, during the Obama administration, this tax code was used by the IRS to prevent tax exempt status being given to conservative groups (Tea Party), while approving liberal leaning organizations. While ample evidence was forthcoming, then FBI Director Comey stated the FBI could find no evidence and therefore no charges would be made. "They" stick together and protect each other.

#28. Eliminate prayer or any phase of religious expression in the schools on the grounds that it violates the principle of "separation of church and state."

This was accomplished by Supreme Court Decisions banning school prayer in 1962 and again in 1963. "They" accomplished this goal very early, which was necessary from their perspective. "They" didn't want any religious influence or morals taught to children in schools. "They" only wanted their viewpoints taught.

#29. Discredit the American Constitution by calling it inadequate, old-fashioned, out of step with modern needs, a hindrance to cooperation between nations on a worldwide basis.

#30. Discredit the American Founding Fathers. Present them as selfish aristocrats who had no concern for the "common man."

#31. Belittle all forms of American culture and discourage the teaching of American history on the ground that it was only a minor part of the "big picture." Give more emphasis to Russian history since the Communists took over.

#32. Support any socialist movement to give centralized control over any part of the culture-education, social agencies, welfare programs, mental health clinics, etc.

#33. Eliminate all laws or procedures which interfere with the operation of the Communist apparatus.

#34. Eliminate the House Committee on Un-American Activities.

This committee was created to investigate potential disloyalty and subversive activities of private citizens, public employees, and organizations suspected of having Communist ties. In 1969, the House changed the committee's name to "House Committee on Internal Security", which was formally abolished in 1975 accomplishing the listed goal. Now who would want to dismantle this committee? The answer is "They", and these were elected politicians.

#36. Infiltrate and gain control of more unions.

#37. Infiltrate and gain control of big business.

#38. Transfer some of the powers of arrest from the police to social agencies. Treat all behavioral problems as psychiatric disorders which no one but psychiatrists can understand [or treat].

#39. Dominate the psychiatric profession and use mental health laws as a means of gaining coercive control over those who oppose Communist goals.

 # 40. Discredit the family as an institution. Encourage promiscuity and easy divorce.

This is another easy one, since the estimated divorce rate in the U.S. today is fifty percent.

#41. Emphasize the need to raise children away from the negative influence of parents. Attribute prejudices, mental blocks and retarding of children to suppressive influence of parents.

#42. Create the impression that violence and insurrection are legitimate aspects of the American tradition; that students and special-interest groups should rise up and use "united force" to solve economic, political or social problems.

#43. Overthrow all colonial governments before native populations are ready for self-government.

#44. Internationalize the Panama Canal.

This was accomplished in 1977 when President Carter signed and gave away the Panama Canal. This very issue launched Ronald Regan into the presidential Republican Primaries in 1976 by opposing the treaty. Candidate Regan said, "We bought it. We built it. We paid for it, and Panama should be told that we intend to keep it." Ronald Regan was right, but President Carter and the progressives gave it away. Why? We did buy the original lease and contract from France, we paid

Columbia and Panama for it, we owned it outright, and by treaty paid for a perpetual lease for the land, we built it at a cost of trillions. Why would America want to *give* it away? Why, because it was on the Communist list of goals and they wanted control and got it, and obviously President Carter was one of the "They."

#45. Repeal the Connally reservation so the United States cannot prevent the World Court from seizing jurisdiction [over domestic problems. Give the World Court jurisdiction over nations and individuals alike.

This is one of the few goals not yet achieved. You better hope it never is.

Chapter 3
(The Debate)

After the participants had read the Communist Manifesto and were pondering their thoughts on the subject, silence filled the room.

It was Dr. Wisscroff that finally broke the silence and said, "You know I'm old enough to remember when the Nikita Khrushchev pounded his shoe on the podium of the United Nations and shouted to the West, 'We will bury you!' I remember that vividly, and I also remember how the West was shocked and also frightened with his audacity. Reading this manifesto drives home the point of his meaning. He wasn't talking about armed combat. They have come a long ways toward this goal ... too far. I'm starting to see the reality of what General Bruner is warning. But, assuming we all agree with his plan, how would we accomplish all these assassinations. We don't have it in us?"

General Bruner said, "I haven't actually told John yet, but our organization, our NAZI Reich, had and probably still do have sleeper cells that can be activated, with his approval of course. These sleeper cells consist of trained assassins and were in place to do this very thing under the previous Supreme Commander. They are highly skilled and can do some of the more difficult kills, but they are not enough for the multitudes needed, not even close. We also have thousands of trained soldiers in the Underworld and trained Resis soldiers that could be utilized if Supreme Commander Meeker authorizes it. They could be sent out on missions."

John instantly said, "No! The NAZI soldiers will remain in the Underworld, and the Resis are a peaceful race, nor should they be involved. We want to keep them that way. But we can discuss the sleeper cells. That might be a good idea. But, General Bruner, regardless of whether we use the sleeper cells or not, they come back to the Underworld afterwards." The general gave a knowing smile and nodded.

A Marine three star general, General Toma said, "We are a delegation representing many more military, ex-military, and a multitude of other patriots. We are talking about trained veterans. We've, I certainly have for sure, been contacted by huge numbers, you wouldn't believe how many, threatening to launch a revolution. They are pissed … really pissed, and they just want some leadership and organization. Many openly offer to kill targets, but need guidance and direction. It's scary, actually, but they seem totally committed and don't seem afraid of any repercussions. I bring this up because they want to get involved, and guided and supported in the right way and seem willing to do this very thing. What I am most concerned with is the secrecy required to accomplish this. The Internet is far too open a venue for secrecy. If we act to support them, the secret will get out, and the targets and enemies will be warned, and we will get shut down and face prison or execution for treason. I guess what I'm saying is there has to be some way of using them, or better said, giving them some focused direction. I just don't know how to do this safely."

Sue Chambers jumped into the conversation and said, "General Bruner, you mentioned in your earlier, shocking statement right after you mentioned assassinating millions, almost as an afterthought that many of us might have missed, that we must take their funds. What did you mean by that?"

General Bruner said, "Secrecy kind of ties into Miss Chamber's question. This is where the Star Children could be a major asset. The Underworld doesn't have the advanced technology to maintain the secrecy required in an operation this massive, nor is it able to steal funds undetected. We can't hack into the necessary websites. But, the Arcadian archive, accessible by Star Children, does have that advanced technology, at least I believe that it does. And to answer your question, taking the funding away from the Communist and elites is as important as eliminating them. In many ways it is more important. Without the dedicated globalists billionaires and corporations funding their organizations, their movement dies. It's like cutting off the blood supply. The workers and leaders must die and the funding that hires new ones must also die. You can't bribe or buy someone off without funds."

Tom was about to speak, but Sue said, "Wait! Can't we accomplish the Coup by concentrating on taking all their funds?"

General Warner was the one that answered, "No that won't work. Far too many roadblocks and counterattack protocols are already funded and in place for the opposition. They will launch these actions automatically, which will include political, legal, and media attacks. Lack of funding would only hamper the secondary attacks."

"I'm beginning to see the logic and necessity of General Bruner's proposal. I have my own reason for coming around to the plan. It was something he said about the casualties. I have seen war far too close. The deaths of war are always among our youth, our sons and daughters pay the price of war, not those that gain profit and power by initiating and declaring war. As military leaders we have witnessed the horrors of battle, the mutilations, blood and guts, and heart-wrenching deaths. In General Bruner's suggestion the ones forcing the conflict are the globalist with an agenda, or as General Bruner points out, Communists that want to destroy America from within. For once I would like to see a war, if war is inevitable, where the proper people die and not the innocent patriots. Once you get past the horror of accepting mass assassinations in a war, it begins to make sense. I have been convinced, and I'm beginning to prefer this form of war." Several of the generals and admirals of the delegation offered solemn and thoughtful nods, even Sue.

Tom said, "Thank you for those comments, general."

General Bruner said, "Yes, General Warner is beginning to understand. They have had decades to plan and create contingency plans and have them currently in place and funded by laws created to drive and protect their agenda. All they have to do is push the right buttons. That's why the button pushers must be eliminated."

Tom continued, "Now, what I was going to say earlier, I thought technology might come up in this discussion. That's why I invited Berta. Berta has excelled in exploring the Arcadian archive. She is our self-taught Star Child technology expert. Berta, do you have any thoughts on this technology requirement being discussed?"

Berta said, "The Arcadian archive is a wealth of knowledge, including advanced technology. I'm sure this technology exists within the archive. I just have to seek it out and download it into my mind. I can develop a team of Star Children to research this technology and implement it, but it could take a few hours. Give me a little time, and I can report back my progress."

Fred, another one of the original six Star Children and mate to Berta quickly said, "I will help you, Berta." Berta smiled.

Admiral Jones said, "Excuse me, Berta, but how will you be able to research this highly advanced technology in just a few hours, and please, can you explain what this Arcadian archive is?"

Berta smiled and said, "Admiral Jones, I understand your skepticism. Let me explain some things about Star Children that you may not know. Our DNA has been genetically engineered to be a combination of both Arcadian and Human, and if you don't already know, Arcadians are an advanced alien race that migrated to Earth about a thousand years ago. Basically we, Star Children, are Arcadians in Human bodies. You met a holographic image earlier of an Arcadian, Mr. Mum, in their original form. Unfortunately, all the Arcadians in their original form have pass, but they created and left the Star Children to live on for them and left us all their recorded archive. We have the Arcadian mental powers, which I will not go into, but one such ability comes with the exceptionally increased intellect. We can mentally interface with the Arcadian archive, which is all the stored knowledge of the ancient Arcadian race over millennia and much of the Human knowledge absorbed since arriving here on Earth years ago. This, of course, is virtually everything. You would relate to the Arcadian archive as a supercomputer. That is as close of a Human comparison as possible, but the Arcadian archive is far beyond any Earth technology. Just accept that a Star Child can instantly download information directly into our subconscious mind from the archive. As an example, not so long ago I was a slave in the Underworld and functionally illiterate. Today I have the equivalent of doctorate level Earth degrees in fourteen fields and in multiple languages, plus additional, accumulated knowledge in fields unknown to Earth's academia. Many of the Star Children are likewise educated. I have learned this knowledge through the Arcadian archive. If the technology we desire exists in the archive, which I am sure that it does, I have instant access to that knowledge. Once my mind owns this knowledge I will then be able to apply it to the needs of the current discussion. This is why I can report back so quickly."

Jane Turret laughed at the admiral's astonished looks and said, "Welcome to the Sanctuary and the world of Star Children. This is why we remain isolated, the world has a hard time accepting us and our abilities. It frightens them."

Admiral Jones laughed at himself and said, "I have to admit that I am one of them. This scares the hell out of me, but I'm thankful that we are hopefully working on the same side."

General Warner switched the subject and said, "If we could find a way to bring the NSA into this group I think we would have a major head start toward our goals."

Surprisingly, a previously silent 4-Star Army general, his name tag said, General Barney, said, "As many of you know, the NSA and Cyber Security currently falls under my purview, for the time being anyway. The new president and his Secretary of Defense will soon replace me with one of his socialist. As many of you also know, I am a patriot and one of the initiators of this group of like-minded patriots. But, my tenure is tentative at best."

"After listening to this discussion I'm going to make a bold statement that to most of the military delegation will be surprising. If we have the ability, I think we need to completely bypass the NSA and keep them out of our planned Coup." Surprise registered around the table, even the Sanctuary group.

"Now, let me explain why I'm saying this. U.S. Government agencies have been heavily infiltrated

71

by Marxist, as General Bruner calls them Communist, for decades. This is even more accurate when it comes to the NSA. The NSA organization is totally corrupted. Taking over the NSA in secret will be almost impossible to accomplish. Additionally, the NSA will be, without doubt, the number one target of suspicion by the anarchists when it comes to cybersecurity. The NSA is very powerful and skillful in cybersecurity, and what we are proposing would be considered almost impossible to accomplish without them. I say, let them take the brunt of the criticism and investigations, since it's beginning to look like we can do what is needed without them…even better. It would take quite some time, if ever, for the NSA to overcome any suspicion. Those higher echelon progressives might realize the NSA was not involved, but we can keep the suspicion alive by planting incriminating evidence. This leads me to the next reason for my statement."

"If we can successfully hack into the NSA in secret, we can issue orders to their field operatives for assassination teams to be deployed, and, yes, the NSA does have hit teams. If the NSA orders and preforms many of the assassinations they own the Coup, and the suspicions will be confirmed, and any investigator will not even bother to look further. We can gain a sizable team of assassins, and we remain invisible."

"Anyway, these are my initial thoughts on the subject, food for thought."

General Bruner actually applauded and said, "I totally agree with your assessment. I like the way you think."

General Warner said, "I think I do, too, but how does the Sanctuary feel about this?"

Tom Bradley sat silent for a while then said, "I'm not sure. We must talk about this among ourselves. I will say, however, something Mr. Mum and I alluded to earlier. Arcadians do have a fault in that we are benevolent by nature. We are not devious and manipulative. What you see is who we are. Knowing this initially, we sought out Dr. Wisscroff as our mentor to advise us in these matters. Dr. Wisscroff, would you care to respond?"

Dr. Wisscroff said, "Well, like you, Tom, I need to think about all I have heard today. It's a lot to process, but I think we need more information, mostly from Berta. We can make better decisions once we know what Berta and her team can provide. It all seems to come down to technology. Let's adjourn, get some rest, have a good meal, and meet again tomorrow."

General Bruner said, "Wait! Since we are researching technology, let me bring up something we discussed earlier. We do run the risk of a potential attack from America and other countries here at the Sanctuary and the Underworld if our secret gets out. I think we need to consider additional protection. I would like us to consider placing a weaponized satellite in stationary orbit above us to protect us from any kind of aerial attack, especially a nuclear missile or biological."

"We have production facilities in the Underworld capable of building a satellite, and the Sanctuary has the ability, through your advanced saucers to launch it or them; but we needs the required technical plans. I ask that Berta and her team also research these technical plans."

Mr. Mum surprised everyone when he materialized above the conference table again. He said, "We agree with this plan. The Arcadians had similar plans in the works before Earth diseases decimated our race. We never completed the operation, but we did anticipate the need and designed and built several satellites for monitoring and as weapons for possible protection. Unfortunately, they are stored on our Mother Ship now imprisoned under a thousand feet of ice shelf. Mr. Bradley and Miss Chambers, you already know about the existence of our Mother Ship, although you never inquired about the details. It can be reached with difficulty, but like finding the entrance to the Sanctuary, it will require a team of Star Children. Tina is the only remaining Star Child with the premonition or sixth sense ability to detect the beacon on the Mother Ship. All the other younger ones with that specific ability were assassinated by the NAZIs." At that statement and reminder, all eyes turned toward General Bruner.

As typical for a psychopath, there was no remorse in General Bruner. He just said, "That was war, and deaths happen in war." He did, however, remain silent, choosing not to aggravate the Star Children further.

Mr. Mum continued, "I recommend that you find the mother ship and activate it. Release it from a thousand years of imprisonment in the ice shelf and launch the satellites. If this potential battle should occur and fail, the Mother Ship could also be used for the Star Children to escape Earth and relocate elsewhere."

Tom said, "We will organize a search team and honor your wishes, Mr. Mum. When we put together a team we will come see you for additional information."

John Meeker said, "Now, before we leave, I must rein in my Underworld associate. General Bruner is utilizing some mental manipulative powers unique to his altered race to potentially influence your thoughts. I brought him to advise and consult, not control you. Any decision made here must be based upon facts and mutual agreement. If you change your mind, make sure it is your own well thought out decision and not manipulation. This is the main reason we must keep the Underworld segregated from the outside world. So, keep a clear and reasoned mind." General Bruner simply nodded his understanding of his instructions.

The meeting adjourned and everyone gravitated toward the cafeteria for one of the Marine Combat Cooks' tantalizing meals. The military delegations members congregated together in a corner of the cafeteria to talk among themselves, and Dr. Wisscroff cornered General Bruner, John Meeker, and Jane Turret to a separate corner table. Tom knew what the military delegation would most likely be talking about, but he had no idea what Dr.

Wisscroff was up to, and his mind was blocked. Tom and Sue took a table, also separate, and Berta and Fred joined them. It appeared that the discussions were far from over.

Berta said, "Should we get involved in learning about the Mother Ship?"

Sue said, "No. You have a far more important task learning the Arcadian IT technology. So much is hinged upon your research in that area."

Berta said, "It will take a few hours, since I'm calling out a team of Star Children to assist. Fred has already volunteered, but I think I will need maybe ten more. I will pick some of those that were slaves with me in the Underworld, the oldest ones. I think they would have more of a vested interest in the subject matter, since they can better relate to abusers. If we move forward with this operation this team will become heavily involved. I just needed some food before I get started."

"Great. We will all be looking forward to your report tomorrow."

Tom asked Sue, "Do you want to get involved with finding the Mother Ship or should we delegate it?"

"I think we better stay focused on the Coup right now. We need to make sure it is the right thing to do and if we can pull it off. Maybe we can ask Jerry and Mary to take that project on. Like us, they are always together anyway and make a good team we can trust. And, of course, Tina. She will be necessary, like Mr. Mum pointed out."

There were forty Star Children, but Tom and Sue tended to rely on the original team of six. They had fought together and knew each other's strong points, not to mention proven trust. Berta was the exception, but she had, on her own volition, made herself indispensable as an archive sponge for knowledge. She had excelled in technical solutions during the Alien War, which helped them win. Now Berta would be their technical authority on cyber security, and a lot would hinge on her opinion and abilities.

After Berta and Jerry left, they remained alone. Sue said, "I'm not sure what John was referring to about General Bruner's manipulative mental ability. I'm starting to come around to accepting the general's solution. Do you suppose the general was using that influence on me?"

"No, John once explained the NAZI's power. It's not quite like what we have, and it doesn't work on Star Children, only normal humans. If you are beginning to agree with him it is because of what he is saying and the facts, not the way he is saying it or any external powers used. John says it's real, and that is the main reason the NAZIs can't be allowed outside of the Underworld to interface with the rest of the world. They forcefully dominate by their nature and would begin to control and manipulate the average human, and John says they can be really cruel, which of course we have seen."

Sue smiled and said, "General Bruner has radical ideas and certainly is not winning friends. His personality has a lot to be desired." Tom laughed, understanding.

Tom said, "John brought him for his knowledge and experience, knowing he lacked in social skills. I

77

must admit that the general has done his homework and truly understand the situation we find ourselves involved in." Sue nodded in agreement.

Tom sent a telepathic message to Jerry, Mary, and Tina asking them to volunteer to launch a team to research all they could find concerning the Mother Ship and build a team to go find it and activate it. They all immediately acknowledged, Tina responded with, *"I love to fly. I'm going to be the pilot."*

Sue laughed and said, "Sure, that's what we need, an eleven year old flying the Mother Ship. I can see us doing flips and flying upside down." Tom grinned.

Chapter 4
(The Decision)

The cafeteria was packed early the next morning with people filling up on food and strong Marine coffee for another busy day, and all the participants of their scheduled meeting were there. They were all eager to hear Berta's report and waited for her to leave. When Berta got up to dump her tray, half of the cafeteria jumped up to do the same and followed her out. Tom and Sue were no exception.

When all were seated in the archive conference room, including Berta's ten new assistances, Tom said, "I think all here are waiting for your report, Berta, so I will just turn it over to you. What did you find out?"

A serious Berta said, "Well, I found out that the Arcadians were very smart, and their, ours now, technology was/is exceptionally advanced for Earth's standards. Earth's cyber technology is primitive in comparison. The bottom line to my report is that we can do anything we want to do in cyber security without detection or being hacked, and we can hack any cyber technology that exist today on Earth without being discovered." Cheers rang out in the conference room.

General Barney said, "Are you aware of how sophisticated the NSA has become? They are huge and probably the most powerful and advanced cyber operation in the world. We certainly don't want to underestimate them."

Berta smiled and said, "General Barney, we have already hacked the DOD, NSA, FBI, CIA, DOJ, IRS … all of them, and have already mapped out all the back-doors and secret accesses into the networks and even created our own secure links. We knew before we started that the cyber security was crude at best, and we had no problems at all. We own those networks. Once Mary retrieves the Mother Ship and we can launch the satellites, we will gain access to all the closed networks and have absolute control of cyber operation on Earth."

The befuddled general intelligently said, "No shit? How in the world did you do that?"

"You would not understand the technology. No one on Earth would. Encryption technology proved to be quite easy for us. Suffice to say it is like comparing simple arithmetic to abstract calculus."

Admiral Jones asked, "Do you have a solution to security for the mass communication required for the inquiring patriots and the massive transmission and storage of information?"

"That level of processing will be available with our own satellites in operation. We have a workable procedure we are working on, but it's not perfected yet. But, I see no problem in doing so."

Admiral Jones said, "Correct me if I'm wrong, but are you saying we will be able to accomplish our discussed goals … all of them, and we can move forward in our planning?"

"Yes, I can report to this group that we can accomplish all the discussed technical goals, assuming we agree to move forward."

Berta continued, "On a second issue from yesterdays' discussion, we discovered startling information of the upmost importance. We hacked numerous governments and governments' data locations and researched the hypothesis General Bruner made concerning the release of the COVID virus. The short answer is yes, the virus was created and intentionally released, and we found that a major, secret conspiracy was involved between Communist countries including Russia, China, the World Health Organization (WHO), and many in the US government. The release of the virus was planned, known, timed, and authorized by all involved in order to launch a pandemic to influence and ultimately control the last election. We found substantial, incriminating evidence of this conspiracy. There is no doubt the Communist world conspired to bring down America through a compromised election process and complete their takeover. I can leak this information serendipitously." Tom smiled and nodded.

"Additionally we discovered evidence even more horrifying, if you can believe that, we discovered a top-secret plan, as General Bruner also alluded to, that involves the existence of a weaponized Smallpox virus, and plans are in the works to release it prior to the next election to shut down and corrupt the election process again. What is most horrifying is the fact that the death rate of the weaponized version of this Smallpox virus is projected to be 50 percent. Billions would die from this particularly horrific disease, and those that survived might wish they hadn't. They would be horribly scared. Even more malevolent is the fact that we also discovered there is a vaccine for the weaponized virus that they plan to incorporate into another COVID booster shot, but the distribution plan is selective. They plan to provide it only to their operatives and not to the general populous. Bottom line is that the Communist are planning their own assassination Coup virus in which only the upper echelon will survive. Their perceived problems of overpopulation will be resolved, along with the extermination of millions of American patriots, and they plan all this to happen before the next election."

General Bruner said, "Incredible! I knew something was being planned, but I had no idea of the depth of their scheme. That plan shows pure genius in the planning, even though it's morbidly diabolical. I don't believe even I could have conceived of such a game plan."

Dr. Wisscroff said, "I thought there is a vaccine for Smallpox. That is how Smallpox was eradicated. I myself still have the arm scar of the Smallpox vaccine." As he spoke he absentmindedly rubbed his shoulder.

A previously silent, Admiral Shirley Martin said, "As most of you know I'm the current Surgeon General, and these subjects have been foremost on my mind for years. What you are bringing up about the COVID release we have known for months. We even tried to warn the powers to be, but the embedded Communist operatives in our government and media have ignored and silenced us. The pending Smallpox virus and its release is, however, new, although it has been a major concern due to the horrendous consequences of a new outbreak. The predicted 50 percent death rate makes it even more horrendous. The original 30 to 40 percent death rate was bad enough. Previously even those that survived Smallpox were horribly scared and probably wished they had died. A release of a weaponized version would mean an almost certain extinction of much of the world's population."

"We eradicated the disease with a worldwide vaccine and the last known case of Smallpox was in 1970. Since then the World Health Organization (WHO) declared the disease dead in the 1980s, and we stopped the manufacturing and distribution of the vaccine."

Dr. Wisscroff said, "What about those that have had the vaccine, like me? Are we immunized to the disease, and can we provide the antibodies for more vaccine?"

"Dr. Wisscroff, that has been over 30 years ago. I seriously doubt you or anyone else would have antibodies remaining after that amount of time, and it would take a long time to research and develop a vaccine for an advanced strain of Smallpox, much less manufacture it in volume due to the time factor involved."

"We have fought Mother Nature's diseases and won with many of them, but it's hard to fight against diseases developed as bioweapons. We should have maintained the created vaccines against diseases like Smallpox, polio in enough volume to be distributed, but we have not."

General Bruner asked, "Tell me Berta, when you were in that data site, did you happen to capture the vaccine's formula? It would be nice to have, just in case."

"Sorry, I didn't think of that. I was too shocked at the information we were discovering to think in terms of a solution. We will definitely hack back into the site and gather that information, "

Admiral Martin said, "I'm afraid that would not solve the problem. It will require a culture sample as well."

General Warner said, "Those dirty SOBs. We know they can play dirty, but this is horrible, even for them. Can they be stopped at this point?"

Berta said, "It's not too late. The virus is still being tweaked in China, and vaccine hasn't begun being manufactured in mass. I think we have a little time yet. And, as far as stopping them, if we have our own satellites in orbit we can destroy the lab and data base."

Sue said, "Mr. Mum, are we safe from a biological attack here in the Sanctuary?"

Mr. Mum flashed back into existence and said, "We chose Antarctica for our home in the Antarctic Circle, because the subfreezing temperatures here destroys germs and bacteria that carry Earth's diseases, to which Arcadians had no natural immunities. These diseases eventually destroyed us, but Star Children have the Human genetic markers to defend you. Star Children have the antibodies to fight off the Smallpox virus and many other Earth diseases, but you remain susceptible to their infection on a minor level. The COVID and other diseases created in labs, new diseases or bio weapons, we had no way to anticipate. So, our answer is that we aren't sure about protection from the new viruses. The Sanctuary, however, has technical protection built into the 24 hour lighting that destroys any air transmitted viruses. Having made that statement, the Sanctuary is vulnerable to outside diseases due to outside visitors like the delegation. It might be advisable as a precaution to install a decontamination station at both entrances, should you feel the need. The Underworld has little need to worry, due to the outside temperature and the fact that they don't come and go from there, and they have no visitors."

Admiral Martin said, "Mr. Mum, you mentioned that Star Children have genetic modifications to protect from Smallpox and other diseases. Is it possible to create a vaccine from a Star Child's blood sample?"

"That's an interesting question. Without research I can't answer that question, but the subject has merit. I might suggest that we choose a Star Child to seek out the medical education from our archive and advise us on these matters. I might also suggest you find a human virologist and bring him or her here to work with our Arcadian trained medical expert we will develop. We like the potential benefits to our Star Children and human friends that might be gained."

Tom said, "Thank you for bringing that up. Mr. Mum, as always we will honor your suggestions,"

85

General Warner said, "Can we now decide if we are all in agreement to move forward with the Coup?"

Dr. Wisscroff stood and said, "Tom, Sue, and the rest of you, I think I'm ready to make my comments now." He received a nod from both the leaders. "I've listened to all concerned, and I know that you Star Children value my opinion as your chosen mentor. This responsibility weighs heavy on me, but I'm speaking my personal thoughts. I think we *should* back and support this delegations' request for help. I'm also persuaded by General Bruner's argument for assassinations. Never have I seen more deserving traitorous targets. I'm persuaded that these schemers' actions have been a long-term, concentrated conspiracy to intentionally bankrupt and destroy America from inside our own government. Their goal has obviously been and is the eventual conversion to socialism and the absorption of America into a one-world Communist government rule."

"I have lived my entire, long life in America, and in retrospect, have watched my rights, my values, my God, my money, my vote, and my freedom slowly disappear. Now the socialist are trying to come after my guns, so I couldn't fight back if I wanted to. I for one am tired of watching it happen. It's time to reverse their actions and do something while we still can, assuming we still can. "

General Bruner set up high in his chair with a huge grin on his face, knowing he had been successful; but he remained silent. He knew his time to provide more input would come later, and he was ready.

No one spoke, allowing the total silence of their potential vote weigh on them. Finally,

General Warner said, "Do we want to take a vote?"

Mrs. Wilks stood to get everyone's attention and said, "I know I'm not a Star Child, but I hope I have earned my right to be here as a member of this society and speak my opinion." The Star Children as one nodded their approval. "I also believe, as Dr. Wisscroff has said, that you value my opinion and this also weighs heavy on me. Still, there are facts coming forth about the globalist actions that must be defeated and corrected. I too have lived a long life in America and enjoyed the freedoms our forefathers passed on to us. They fought wars to gain these freedoms and many died to keep them. It galls me to see how far they have come in their agenda and how close they are in achieving them. I know you Star Children are not American. You are independent from the world, but many of you were raised in America and can relate to freedom. It frightens me to even think what America and the world would be like if they complete their goals. America protects you, because they are strong. If they fall under the control of the Communist they will no longer be an ally. I can honestly understand how the patriots in America must feel, because I feel the same way. So, my vote will be to fight them … fight back, remove them, and take back our country."

Tom said, "Colonel Burns, you have earned your place among us. You are one of us, and you have a vote here. We would like to hear your thoughts."

Colonel Burns set up straight and said, "Thank you for your words. I do feel like I belong. We have gone through much together, and I do feel accepted. I have listened intently to the discussion, and I am persuaded to agree with the need and the method for a Coup. I want to thank the military delegation here and those this group represents. It took a lot of courage for them to come here and ask for help. The delegation is in danger if we don't help them. I'm pleased that they bring it to us, because we couldn't accomplish a Coup without them, and they couldn't do it without us. At this table sets the best of both worlds." Many thankful nods rotated around the table from both groups.

Tom said, "Does anyone else wish to speak" Silence continued. Tom pointed to the Dr. Wisscroff setting next to him on his left and said, "Let's start with you and make your vote official and go around the table clockwise." By doing this, Tom ensured that he would have the last vote.

Dr. Wisscroff said, "My vote is yes!"

The vote continued through the military delegation with yes after yes until it reached Berta. Berta sat in silence for a very long moment then said, "With great reluctance I am voting yes."

Mrs. Wilks, Colonel Burns, and the other Star Children present followed Berta's yes vote, including Sue. John and Jane voted yes, and General Bruner followed them with a loud yes, which of course all expected. Some even chuckled. It was all yes votes to Tom, but he was reluctant and said, "I don't want to commit us to war without the full vote of the Sanctuary, meaning the Star Children."

Mr. Mum's image flashed alive above the table and said, "You haven't asked us, the archive of the long dead Arcadians, but we vote yes. We think it is in the best interest of the Sanctuary and our modified race. Additionally, I have linked all the other Star Children telepathically into our discussions here, and they are following our vote. If any disagree and wish to vote no, then speak up now." There were numerous pings acknowledging but nothing negative.

Tom said, "Well, I guess it is unanimous. We go to war, and the Sanctuary and Underworld will join with the military and patriots of America. Now comes the hard part, we have to figure out how to accomplish it."

Chapter 5
(The Targets)

Jerry and Mary had been busy with their own project of exploring and mapping out the vast underground caves under the Sanctuary when they got Tom's message about assigning them the project of finding the Mother Ship. They immediately dropped their project, since it could be completed later and at any time. This new project sounded far more interesting. Jerry and Mary slapped a high-five high in the air showing their enthusiasm. This project seemed very important, and they relished taking on the responsibility. From past experience Tom and Sue knew that Mary was the dominant persona and she would take control of the project, and she immediately did.

Mary said, "We need to bring in Gary and Bridget, and Don and Karen. I'm thinking we should meet at Mr. Mum's dais, his soapbox, and let him guide us as to what we need to know in order to find and operate the Mother Ship." Jerry quickly messaged the Star Children mentioned, plus Tina, and asked them to meet them at Mr. Mum's location. They then flew out of the caves toward the entrance park where Mr. Mum stood sentinel over the Sanctuary.

They all seemed to arrive around the same time and gathered around the ever vigilant image of Mr. Mum. Mr. Mum stared at them and waited.

Mary said, "Mr. Mum we came to find out about the Mother Ship. We didn't know we have a Mother Ship, but we have been tasked to find and activate it. Can you tell us about the Mother Ship and where in the archive to access information about it?"

Mr. Mum focused and said, "Yes, I suggested the need for what you have been tasked with. The Arcadians arrived on Earth in our Mother Ship almost a thousand years ago. The Human race was still in its infancy, and we tried to interface and help them develop. Sadly, we were decimated by Human diseases. In the beginning we numbered in the thousands but were reduced by illness to only a few hundred. We were forced to isolate ourselves to the southern arctic region where there were no Humans or diseases and the frigid temperatures canceled out the germs and bacteria. We discovered this cavern and settled the Mother Ship on the Ross Ice Shelf while we built the Sanctuary. Due to our reduced population we failed to perform the required maintenance, and due to a minor generated heat of the ship, over time the ship slowly sank into the ice and covered over with new snow and ice. It took many years to sink, but it is now estimated to be about a thousand feet deep in the ice, maybe more. It remains fully operational but will be hard to find, since it is so deep. We believe Tina's power is sufficient to detect the beacon if she can get close enough to it. The archive can, however, provide the approximate location."

"As far as the archive, simply look for information titled 'ARC' (Arcadian Relocation

Carrier). That is the English name of the ship, which seemed appropriate at the time of its planning and construction. Later we discovered in the Bible that Noah built an arc to save lifeforms to repopulate Earth, which also seemed appropriate for us."

Mary said, "Thank you Mr. Mum. We will go to the archive and begin our research."

They then proceeded to their individual, informational cubical to begin their access and brain downloads. Even though they were accessing different information, their minds were linked through the archive and what one learned the others learned also. They quickly realized that approaching the archive for research with a team became far more efficient, which knowledge she quickly shared with Berta and the others. After about an hour they had gained all the knowledge about "ARC" that was available. They knew all the design details, operational procedures, history of its travel across the universe, weapon systems, current inventories on board, and the coordinates of its position 980 years previous. Now they would have to find it and reach it. At this point Mary didn't know how they were going to get it out of the ice.

Mary said, "I'm hoping this will be easier to find than when we had to locate the Sanctuary entrance. This time we should be able to use a saucer instead of a heat bubble."

Tina said, "I thought that the heat bubble was fun."

Jerry blurted, "Hell no! It was damn cold. We are going to use a saucer." Tina frowned but nodded.

Mary said, "I guess you have all been listening to the key points of the discussion that's been going on, and it looks like we are going to war. I think the panel will be needing us to give our initial report on the Mother Ship quickly, and as we have discovered, the Mother Ship will be needed. I think we better make the meeting in the morning before we embark on our search." They agreed, and Mary telepathically notified Sue of their intent.

***

When all were gathered in the growing conference room, Tom said, "We have added Mary and Fred's team today. They want to report on their research on the Mother Ship. Mary, you have the floor, so to speak."

Somewhat formally, Mary stood at the podium with a shy Jerry standing far back behind her, the other members of her team having taken seats in an outer ring of borrowed chairs. Mary said, "Good morning all. As mentioned, our team has been tasked to research, find, and activate the lost Mother Ship. We have completed the first phase and discovered many startling facts that can be useful in this coming operation, which we wanted to share with this committee."

"To give you a little background history of 'ARC', which is its official name, was designed and built to relocate the remaining Arcadians to Earth. The home planet was on the verge of extinction, so ARC was built for this purpose. There was only a single Mother Ship ever built, and it encompassed virtually every advanced technology they had invented over millennia, some impossible to

93

describe. ARC is a saucer, and it is massive, much larger than a modern day aircraft carrier. It's capable of faster-than-light speed, required to transport the Arcadians 1,206 light-years to Earth; artificial gravity; invisibility stealth, …"

Tina couldn't resist and interrupted and blurted out, "It's like Star Trek! It has a teleport, warp drive, phasers, energy shields, and photon torpedoes … all of it!" The reaction was mixed: astonishment and amusement.

Mary laughed and said, "Tina, I was getting to all that, but what Tina said is all true. The ARC is a technological marvel of advanced engineering and an awesome war machine, but unfortunately it was the common Earth germ that decimated the Arcadians. The Arcadians could have defended themselves from any attack, even today in Earth's technological age; but they had to escape into the Sanctuary for survival and abandon the ARC. Oh, by the way, the satellites discussed *are* on board, along with many more surprises."

"We, our team, *will* find, release, and activate the ARC; but it might take some time. It is buried deep in the Ross Ice Shelf. We will be able to permanently establish it in orbit for our defense if required. One factor that needs to be reported, which was surprising to us, is that the main Arcadian archive is aboard the ARC. When we are able to activate the ship, this archive will automatically link with the archive here in the Sanctuary and increase its abilities a hundred fold." All, even the Star Children, gasped.

94

Rare for Dr. Wisscroff, he voiced an unintelligible squeal of amazement at this last revelation. He said, "You have got to be kidding me. That is incredible. I am still amazed at the Sanctuary's archive capabilities, and cannot even imagine those capabilities multiplied by a hundred." Mary just shrugged, as if to say, "It is what it is."

Mary continued, "That's about it. We will keep this committee informed about our progress."

Tom said, "Thank you, Mary. We will look forward to your next report. Now, let's start on some of the details and goals we must establish."

Admiral Jones said, "I can bring a team of computer operators and equipment in to do a lot of the detailed work with those patriots that want to get involved."

Berta cut him off by saying, "Thank you, admiral, but I'm afraid we can't use them. This work will all need to be done by Star Children, since we will be using the archive network through mental links. Yes, it is a lot of work, but it's necessary for absolute security. Besides, much of the work will actually be done by the archive, it's almost human in that it is self-aware. What we need from you are the lists of those wishing to become involved from each of you." Berta leaned toward Fred to hear a whispered comment. She nodded and continued. "Actually, we already have those lists and they are being vetted as we speak." At the reaction from the delegation Berta smiled and said. "Yes, we have hacked all your computers, phones, websites and networks, even through all your encryption, fire-walls, and security, and without detection. I told you we could do that, and we did. And before you ask, General Bruner, yes, we retrieved your 'Hit List', and it's being analyzed." General Bruner didn't seem surprise or even care. He must have been eager to provide it.

"Your 'Hit List' numbers over a million people. That's a lot of assassinations to justify. Want to comment about your list?" Berta knew this might take a while, so she sat down.

General Bruner quickly took to the podium to defend his list, "My team has been tracking individuals from all walks of life in America that act to influence and control the country. The main targets we have identified are wealthy, socialist activist funding treasonous movements; but the list included politicians, lawyers, tons of bureaucrats, and media. They are everywhere. But, they all have the same Communist goals: to control politics, media, schools, the legal system, and also the United Nations. We track their affiliations, memberships, campaign donations, voting records, income sources, and supporting actions associated with Communist or anarchist organizations. We have tracked them for decades and keep the list current. As they age, die, retire or become inactive we drop them from the list. The list *was* in the millions, but we have recently revised the list downward, knowing your aversion to the elimination by assassination. Our latest adjusted list numbers closer to a half million of the worst offenders. The current list include:"

Gover
nors   2

State
Attorneys
Generals
15
Secret
aries of
State
17
Lawye
rs
157,000
Gover
nment
Bureaucrat
s 162,000
Politic
ians
62,000
Milita
ry
22,000
Profes
sors –
Teachers
57,000
Judge
s 1,500
Media
82,000
Misc.
50,000
Total
593,534

"The Governors, Attorney Generals, and Secretaries of State on the list were elected, but their campaigns were funded, bought and paid for, and controlled by a multi-billionaire, Marxist activist totally dedicated to a one world government … his. This billionaire and others are also on the list under Misc. We need to take their money and eliminate their influence. One manipulator is the worst offender, but there are others that must go. The politicians mentioned above do the absolute bidding of their sponsor. You have seen the results of their actions in the corrupted last elections. They illegally changed or allowed changes of election laws to allow the corruption of the system and fraudulent election and have continue to support and defend their action."

Sue interrupted and said, "I can support these choices, since the numbers are small. But you are talking huge number for lawyers and bureaucrats. How can you justify these huge numbers?"

General Bruner sighed and said, "It never ceases to amaze me how citizens of America can see the facts staring them in the face and not see their enemy. The citizens give too much authority to their elected officials. Far too many have confidence that the government knows what it's doing. Unfortunately, they do know what they are doing, but it's not what they were elected to do. Since we are talking about lawyers, let me offer a single example: the National Lawyer Guild has membership numbers in the millions … do you hear me? Millions! It's publicly known as a Communist organization, which is also known as the *'legal mouthpiece of the Communist Party'*. Look it up on the Internet. They don't even try to hide it. America's own FBI, back when it was still free America, tried to get Congress to declare the National Lawyer Guild a subversive organization ... several times actually. Congress refused to do so. I wonder why? Remember Goal #33. *(Eliminate all laws or procedures which interfere with the operation of the Communist apparatus).* This is a good example."

"Our team approached the evaluation of lawyer members in a reasonable manor, however. Out of millions, we narrowed the list down to 157,000. The majority of the lawyers were corrupt but not horrendously bad, but far too many were. These are the ones attacking the legal system. Remember Goal #16. *(Use technical decisions of the courts to weaken basic American institutions by claiming their activities violate civil rights).* They are the organizations forcing these technical decisions in the courts. These must go."

"Corrupt government bureaucrats are easily placed and embedded. As a Communist operative gains increased status and authority it is easy for them to fill employment spots below them with like-minded workers. The higher the position, the higher the level of corruption goes; and remember, this has gone on for decades. Also, since they also control the unions, it is difficult to expunge them once they are employed. They remain employed, even after a change of administration, to continue their subversive intervention."

"Politicians? Really? Do you really question the need to eliminate many of them? I remind you of Goal # 15 *(Capture one or both of the political parties)*. Congress is heavily embedded with socialist. They have taken over one party completely and much of the other, but we can't take them all out or they won't have a quorum to make or change laws to correct any of these problems. All we can do is take out the worst and hope the others will get the point."

"The military? Socialists have been embedded over the years, and they cause much damage. I would like the military delegations here to carefully review my list. They may even have additions. But, I think you will find my list would closely match yours, and your confirmation would add credibility to my other categories."

"Professors and teachers are a key target, but not absolutely required for the initial Coup. Still, they might as well be included in our list now in case there is only one wave of assassinations. I refer you to Goal # 17 *(Get control of the schools. Use them as transmission belts for socialism and current Communist propaganda. Soften the curriculum. Get control of teachers 'associations. Put the party line in textbooks)*. They are teaching and indoctrinating your children with the Communist doctrine, rewriting history, and producing the next generation of home grown Communist. This category is greatly dominated by placed socialist. Again, we are targeting only the worst"

"The entire legal system has come to a halt. Very little gets done. Goal *(#16. Use technical decisions of the courts to weaken basic American institutions by claiming their activities violate civil rights*). Liberal judges challenge any new law that doesn't conform to the socialist agenda. The potential law is declared unconstitutional even though the majority of the voters approve and pass the law or referendum. The will of the people is reversed by corrupt judges that act to legislate from the bench. Once a law is declared unconstitutional the law passes from court to court. At worst the ruling stands and the law is killed, and at best the law is delayed, sometimes for years. The corrupt courts and judges must be purged, including the Supreme Court. But, we have not targeted any Supreme Court judges in this list simply because any replacement must be presented by the current liberal president. It would do no good to eliminate a Communist Supreme Court Judge just to be replaced with another. Now, having said this, your previous president's original election was a big surprise to the globalist agenda, and he disrupted and reversed much and replaced many of the judges, including three Supreme Court judges. Had President Thompson not been elected they would have completed their takeover of America. This is why the Communist pulled out all the stops and attacked the election system to steal the last election, which would have reelected President Thompson in a landslide victory. That would have destroyed their movement, or delayed it for many years."

"The majority of the media, both print and television, has become nothing more than propaganda to support the socialist agenda. Goal #20 (Infiltrate the press) & Goal *(#21 Gain control of key positions in radio, TV, and motion pictures)*".

"There are numerous targets that fall under the Misc. category which include all of the alphabet three letter government agencies, CEOs and executives of subversive corporations, big-tech social media executives, wealthy supporters, politicized religious leaders, anarchists groups. It actually amazes me that these anarchist groups are an exact copy of the NAZI's Brown Shirt thug groups in Germany we used to intimidate and destroy our opposition when we took over prior to WW-II. America fought a war but learned nothing from it. America can't see the repeat of history happening in front of them. Well, maybe America *is* now beginning to see."

"The list goes on. Do you really need me to go on? I think you get the gist of the composition of the Hit-List." He didn't wait for questions and took his seat, indicating he was finished.

Sue said, "That's a very detailed report, General Bruner, and we thank you for providing such a detailed list. Please understand that with the seriousness of the discussed pending action we must not rush into action without considering all the ramification of our actions. If we proceed in support of this assassinations Coup the results will be totally irreversible. This brings me to something that was said earlier by our youngest Star Child. Tina said that the Mother Ship had the ability to teleport. Instead of assassinating, could we teleport the targets on to the Mother Ship and take them somewhere else?" Heads began shaking violently around the table, and General Bruner threw up his hands in exasperation.

Tom knew Sue wasn't dumb, far from it, maybe a little naive. She was smart and purposely forcing the discussion toward the negative side to pressure all the members to face her concerns and add to the discussion and commit. She probably hoped to hear alternative plans by forcing the discussion, but he saw no alternative solutions.

General Warner jumped up and said, "No! We can't do that. We are talking about over a half million people. The numbers are far too excessive for an operation like that. Additionally, there is nowhere we could put them that would remain secret. The word would get out, and secrecy is our primary goal here. Only the Star Children could pull that off, and the Sanctuary would become the world's target. I'm definitely against that option."

Dr. Wisscroff said, "I agree. Our actions must remain totally secret. I also agree that there is no place on Earth we could put them where they would not be found."

Sue smiled and said, "We could put them somewhere *not* on Earth." She was met with some very shocked stares. "We could put them under the Earth, like maybe the Underworld. There is no communications or escape out of there, and they would be unable to force their will or ideology on the NAZIs there. Earlier General Bruner was complaining about not having enough workers. This might work out well for him and their community."

General Bruner began grinning and said, "Now that was a surprise. I didn't see that coming, but the idea is worth discussing. Possibly we could take some of them, the younger ones with skills that can work; but we could not handle the sheer volume of the numbers listed. I do see a partial compromise if John approves. It's his decision."

Berta forcefully said, "I would never agree to establish slavery again in the Underworld. Remember, I was a slave there, and it was horrible."

John said, "Interesting suggestion, and Berta, I would never again allow slavery in the Underworld. If we do this, their lives might be hard, but it would be better than death. We can consider it and keep an open mind on the subject, but General Bruner and others back in the Underworld and I will have to do some planning. Let us come back to this subject as we near the final plan of action."

Tom said, "I think it's time to stop this meeting and break up in groups and get some actual work done on planning the details. We can meet again tomorrow."

After the meeting John and Jane went to the cafeteria to relax and refresh. They both looked surprised to see General Bruner eating with the other admirals and generals. What surprised them most was the fact that they all seemed to be getting along well. The American military delegation and the NAZI being civil to each other seemed previously unlikely.

During their meal Jane looked thoughtful at John and said, "What did you really think about Sue's idea about the Underground?"

John looked around to make sure no one was close enough to hear, lowered his voice and almost whispered, "It's got some merit on a limited basis, but Sue is a bit naive about the raw volume of people involved. I understand her concern, but it's not realistic. Basically I agree with General Bruner, the Underworld couldn't possibly feed that many more. Like many, I have mixed emotions about all the potential deaths, but I'm persuaded to move forward."

Jane said, "Yeah, that's the way I see it, too."

Chapter 6
(The ARC)

Jerry, Mary and the team were excited to get started. They knew the importance of their task. The team took one of the saucers and exited down the cave and out under the ice shelf and traveled north to the open ocean where they rose above the ice. They then traveled back over the ice to where the Marines guarded the tunnel leading down to the entrance to the Sanctuary. This is where the military delegation gained access to the Sanctuary, and their plane remained parked near the descending vertical ice tunnel, but it was camouflaged to appear to be just more ice. The assumption they were following was that the Mother Ship must have been parked near the Sanctuary entrance as it was being built, but as Tina searched for the beacon signal she registered nothing at all, not even a faint sniff. For the next few days they began spiraling out from the Marine camp until they had covered a distance of a hundred miles in diameter, still nothing. Worry settled on them like a weight, knowing that everyone was depending on them.

Jerry said, "Damn, Tina are you watching and listening carefully?" Tina ignored him out of aggravation at being belittled. Jerry changed his attitude and continued, "Before, when we searched for the Sanctuary beacon, you saw a red, flashing lights and heard it, right?" Tina nodded. "I wonder what we are doing wrong. We must have passed over it by now."

Bridget said, "Could it be the saucer is shielding the signal? We know the saucer has shielding."

Mary laughed and said, "Anything is possible. Certainly, we didn't have a saucer when we searched for the Sanctuary. Maybe you are right. Tina, you might get your wish of searching in a bubble like you wanted to." Tina smiled.

Tina formed her protection and heat bubble and started again, flying and tracing the same pattern. At the end of several more days of slowly searching her spiraled pattern she still hadn't detected a signal. As she floated back toward the Marine complex dejected, she had a sudden inspired idea. Maybe the ARC was just too deep in the ice to detect the signal, and maybe they had been correct in believing the ARC had been parked by the entrance. Tina suddenly shot down the ice tunnel toward the Sanctuary entrance several hundred feet to the bottom. If the ARC had sunk down to a depth of thousand feet or more in the ice, and if it was parked where they thought it should be parked, going down the tunnel would reduce the distance, therefore the resistance blockage from the ice, separating her from the ARC. It worked! She detected a very slight beeping tone and could see a faint red glow off to the North and down. She immediately telepathically transmitted her success. She was rewarded with telepathic pings in return. Tina shot to the ice surface and found her team already inside the Marine complex having coffee.

The team quickly encircled her with hugs and pats on the back.

Mary said, "Congratulations, Tina. Well done. That was a great idea you had going down the tunnel."

Gary said, "Can we approach the ship from the tunnel? Is it close enough? It would save a lot of tunneling."

Tina thought for a moment and said, "Well, apparently it's closer than from the top, since I got a signal down there and not from the top. So I guess we can, but its location is deeper."

Mary said, "That's great. I'll report to Sue that we have located the ARC. They will be happy to know that phase one of our project has been accomplished."

***

The daily meetings continued for several days without any significant obstacles or major accomplishments either. Mostly the concentration remained in separate groups nailing down details. Much hinged upon Berta and her team, and the admirals and generals tried to help, encourage, and tactfully direct, with little success. Berta's team accepted the advice and asked a lot of question about people, companies, locations, concerning the "Hit List"; but the complex technology required processing through the Star Children and archive. The members of the delegation were eager and willing but limited.

As Tom called the daily meeting to order, Sue was the first to respond and said, "We have just gotten some very good news from the Mother Ship team. They have located the ARC. It turned out to be a time-consuming task, but it has been located. There remains the arduous task of reaching it, then extracting it from over a thousand feet of solid ice. It won't be easy, but locating it was the most important part." Cheers rang out.

Jane spoke up, "Thanks, Sue. That is good news for sure. I have especially worried about that. I really want ARC operational. I hope we don't need the extra protection, but if we do, ARC could save us. I'm worried about outside interest getting involved while the US is in turmoil from the Coup, namely from Russia and China. We all realize those are our strongest antagonist, and they are both Communist countries. If they both or either move against us when America is weak they could still accomplish the same goal of taking over control of America." Jane let that sink in, then said, "As you may or may not know, I was the personal interrupter for Russian President Pramin before I discovered I was a Star Child. I believe I still have some influence with him, if it becomes necessary. I might still be able to intervene if a conflict threatens, but having ARC backing me up would be greatly comforting."

General Warner said, "I don't believe any of us knew that about you." He looked around and saw only shaking heads. "That is good to know. It truly could be beneficial in certain circumstances, but I caution you not to bring the subject up with him and let our secret involvement be known. Part ... well all, of our security plans are for the Sanctuary and us to remain invisible to all. Russia and China must never know of your/our involvement, of any of our participation."

Jane somewhat annoyed by the general's patronizing, said, "I understand that fully, general. The Sanctuary has more to lose than anyone, but I bring this option up as a contingency plan. But, since you brought it up, what exactly can you military leaders actually do toward this Coup? Maybe it's time to share details."

Indignantly, General Warner said, "We and everyone under us accepting our leadership are putting our lives at risk if we fail. We will do whatever it takes to succeed, but specifically we intend to ignore any orders from any remaining, compromised, or controlling elite and mobilize against them. We intend to immediately take charge of the military and lock down Congress, the Pentagon, and the major agencies that could resist. We don't currently represent the entire military, but we are comfortable that we control the majority of it. And, once the "Hit List" is triggered to remove the corrupted and controlled ones, we believe we can control all branches and commands. We believe there will be little resistance from anyone, with the major Communist players gone."

"We also hope to be able to work with Berta's team to vet and develop the patriots' termination team. Like I said, our necks are on the line here. We believe this is a substantial contribution, but if you need more from us, all you have to do is ask. Again, we are totally committed."

Tom quickly filled the momentary silence, and said, "Thank you both for your enthusiastic comments and concerns, but we are a team of dedicated members. Let's all remember that, and let's move on now to other subjects. Berta, can you give us an update on the IT aspects?"

Berta said, "We are still working on setting up a secure network for interfacing with the patriots. This is proving to be a difficult undertaking, because of the sheer volume of potential members and the absolute security necessary. The more members we have, the greater the risk of a leak, and any leak could spell disaster for all of us. The existing Internet technology is limiting, but it will be easier when our satellites are deployed. But, in either case the leak worry is concerning. We'll talk more on this in some of the next meetings."

"We are considering trying to limit the numbers of patriot members in the network for the wet work, as in the actual assassinations, and try to utilize more assets from the NAZI cells and teams from the NSA we can control."

It was Admiral Jones that interrupted, "Berta, let me remind you that this Coup is an American Coup. It must be, and must be seen by everyone, primarily as an overwhelming uprising of the citizens, which in point of fact it is. Also, keep in mind that these patriots are mad ... very mad. They have reached the point of no return, and this uprising in America will happen whether we are involved or not. It's these patriots that need to be directed in a common and coordinated strategy or they will erupt on their own, and probably in unanticipated or unadvisable directions. They will accept direction but not a plan where they are not

111

involved. The more members we are directing, the less the odds of an unexpected eruption of defiance. I'm saying we can't restrict them, we can only direct them. This is their revolution. Am I making sense to you?" At that, heads nodded among the delegation.

Berta said, "Very well. Yes, we understand and thank you for pointing that out. You understand them better than we do, living isolated. We will just have to solve the technical problems."

General Bruner stood and said, "This might not be as difficult as you think. Now, before you all start screaming at me again, hear me out. I would suggest you use mind control through audio only, that way there is no digital record that could compromise the operation. The Underworld doesn't have the technology for this, but with some thought and research I believe the Sanctuary just might. Use the mind control power you have to ensure security is maintained. I'm not saying make the network members zombies or anything close. Use mind control to control security only. Like hypnosis, make it impossible for the hearer to breach security. If this mind control signal could be modulated, encrypted and injected within the initial audio contact, you could establish the absolute rules of security you develop. The signal could be delivered through a PC or cell phone with self-destruct, if necessary, instructions of the message also installed. In the unlikely event that an unauthorized person heard the message, they would not be able to share it with another, because the mind control security would be installed within their subconscious mind.

112

Berta, can you embed those mind control instruction in an audio signal?"

The highly educated and incredibly intelligent Berta, for once, seemed genuinely shocked and said, "That is a fantastic idea. Why didn't I think of it?"

Mr. Mum, believing this was a real question, flashed into existence and said, "It's because you do not have a devious and manipulative mind like the Underworld NAZIs." Several of the Star Children laughed out loud.

General Warner asked, "Do you Star Children have that kind of power?"

"Yes, Star Children have many powers, including mind reading and mind control, which we usually rigidly control when we are among humans. The Underworld human race also have this power on a limited basis, but they freely wield their power. That is why they remain sequestered in the Underworld. Unlike us, they can't be trusted to restrict its use." General Bruner just smiled.

"General Bruner's suggestion is actually a great idea. My team and I must experiment and develop a method of converting these mental controls into an audio frequency we can use to modulate them into our transmission. But, I believe this to be possible. If successful, this would solve our security concerns." Berta's team became animated, grasping the implications of this possibility.

Mrs. Wilks raised her hand for attention and when Tom acknowledged her, said, "I've been thinking about the reaction of the populous from all these sudden deaths. Their reaction would probably be like our original distaste. America is not Israel where deaths like these planned are common place. Americans are not used to terrorist attacks, certainly not on this level. Their reaction will be horrific. What if we begin a series of news releases prior to the Coup providing some of the information we have been discussing and start turning public opinion toward a Coup. If the general populous knew what we now know, they would demand a Coup."

General Warner said, "Mrs. Wilks, that is an excellent idea, unfortunately it will not work. Many on our side have been trying to do that for years, but the mainstream media is already corrupted. Our news and evidence falls on deaf ears and gets no traction, and the public doesn't get to see or hear it. The corrupted media will immediately silence our reports and release False News taking the complete opposite spin. We have gotten nowhere with this approach, and we will not until the Coup has purged the corrupted infiltrators."

Berta chimed in saying, "I also believe any attempt to elicit a favorable response from the public prior to completion of the Coup might provide a warning to our targets. We want them lulled into believing that all is well with their takeover. We want their guard down, so to speak."

Tom said, "Mrs. Wilks, thank you for making that observation. It does have merit, but I think we must put any action of that kind on hold. Maybe we can discuss it again later." Mrs. Wilks nodded her understanding.

***

Security had no longer been needed in the archive conference room, but Colonel Burns continued to attend. When he learned of the success of Mary's team in locating the Mother Ship, he immediately found his way up through the Sanctuary access tunnel into the Marine security facility guarding it. The colonel had spent so much time within the controlled constant 75 degree temperature that he had forgotten how cold it was outside. His first mission upon exiting the elevator was to find a foul weather coat to keep from freezing. Finally warm again, he found the Star Children team having coffee with his Marine squad. He could tell they were happy and excited, as well they should be.

Colonel Burns said, "Congratulations kids. You have done well. What comes next, and how can we help?"

When they explained the logistics of the problem to reach the ARC, the colonel said, "Yeah, I see the problems. Maybe we can help with a team with blow torches to melt a tunnel through the ice, but that would certainly create other problems with steam and melted ice. It sounds like you will need ventilation assistance at the top to vent the steam and pumps to vacate the water. Since your planned shaft is slopping downward, melting water will be the real problem. It sounds like it will be a long tunnel, too." After a moment of thought he said, "Have you located the ship from underneath the ice shelf? You said it is deep in the ice shelf. Maybe it's closer from underneath. If so, you might want to consider opening a shaft from underneath. The

115

melting water would flow down into the ocean as long as it is above sea level."

Mary said, "We hadn't considered that approach. That might be an excellent idea. I doubt, however, that the ARC is above sea level, because it is deep in the ice, and 90 percent of the shelf is underwater. Still, I think we can work with that. What do you think, guys?" They were nodding agreement. "If that approach is feasible and works, we might also release ARC out the bottom. Once we gain access, all we would have to do is heat the hull and let the weight of the ship sink it out the bottom. It might take some time to sink out the bottom, but the water would flow back in the space above the ship and freeze again. Problem solved."

Bridget said, "Let's try it. All we have to do is get under the ice in the saucer and fire our laser at low intensity toward ARC until we melt a hole large enough in the ice for us to reach the ship entrance hatch."

Tina said, "Wait. The hole will be full of water. How will we get there?"

Jerry said, "Silly, we will send you in that bubble you like. You can just fly up the hole and open the hatch and turn the heater on." Tina frowned and the others laughed, but basically that's what it amounted to.

Mary said, "Seriously though, it all depends on if Tina can detect the beacon from underneath. I guess that is the next obstacle. Let's give it a try. Colonel, did you want to go with us? It's your idea after all." He just shrugged, as if to say, "Sure, why not?".

The now overly, motivated team immediately left for their saucer and zoomed over the ice and plunged into the open ocean and under the ice cap. Their destination was very near, actually to, the underground Sanctuary entrance. When they reached the coordinates of the topside entrance tunnel Tina began her search for the beacon by steering them north in the approximate direction she located the beacon before. The results were almost immediate, even within the saucer.

Tina said, "I hear it and see it, and the signal is strong. We must be much closer than we were above. I think the ARC is fairly close to the bottom." She steered them until she was looking straight up. "We are here! Let's get started."

Karen, the eighth member of the team, said, "Before we do, I thought we should discuss any potential damage to ARC from our laser, should we strike it directly. I doubt ARC has any defense actively operating. We certainly don't want to destroy it trying to save it."

Mary said, "I think Bridget solved that problem earlier when she suggested using the laser at a lower intensity. I'm doubtful that we can do that, but we *can* expand the focus of the beam to maybe ten feet wide, which would prevent any narrowly focused beam that would do much damage. That would work for our tunnel size as well, and it makes good sense. As an extra precaution we should do the tunnel extraction in stages. Once we get close, we can go up the tunnel and do the last few feet ourselves and locate the hatch."

117

Mary adjusted the laser focus and fired the beam directly up into the floor of the ice. Their view immediately filled with churning and boiling water mixed with air bubbles released from the melting ice. The first thing they noticed was the boiling water continued to melt the tunnel, expanding the tunnel width significantly. Wide enough to nudge the saucer higher into the widening tunnel. The process continued like that for several hours and rising over a hundred feet into the ice. From time to time Tina would make minor adjustments in direction, but for the most part, the tunnel looked completely vertical as they looked down.

When they passed the three hundred foot elevation things changed. The saucer emerged from the water into open, steamy air. They stopped the process to evaluate. They had to wait for a while to let the steam dissipate and their visibility improve.

When the view cleared, Tina said, "We are close, because the signal is strong."

Jerry bellowed, "I see it! Look!" He pointed. "There! See that dark shape in the ice? I don't hear anything, but I see the red, flashing beacon." They all stared where Jerry pointed.

Unfortunately, once they emerged from the water, the boiling water stopped melting and expanding the tunnel. They were as high as they could go with the saucer in the tunnel without potentially damaging the Mother Ship with the laser, but they had room to work on their own outside the saucer.

Colonel Burns said, "I don't think we are above sea level. We must have built up some air pressure

118

released from the melting ice. When you go out, make sure you maintain breathing protection in case the water level rises."

Jerry said, "We will protect ourselves with personal protection bubbles, like Tina used, in case the water rushes back in. We can project heat through it." The colonel nodded.

Karen and Bridget remained inside to maneuver their saucer if necessary, while Tina, Mary, Jerry, Don, and Gary exited from the bottom hatch and floated up as far as they could and began projecting heat. The ice began to bubble and flow down in growing streams, and the air filled with thick steam. The visibility greatly diminished, but their enhanced vision allowed them to view their progress. The hull of the ship became more apparent as the ice melted and flowed down the tunnel. The red, flashing, light was clearly visible to all now and became the target direction. Soon the beacon was exposed and they began spreading out, searching for and clearing the hatch. They found a hatch edge and followed the seam, which turned out to be rectangular in shape about 50'X75'. All the ice was finally removed from the hatch, and they made sure there was enough cleared space on either side for it to open. They then gathered at the beacon, which they knew to be the opening latch.

Mary said, "I did not receive any data on how to open the hatch. Do any of you know of any instructions?" Apparently none of the others had the answer, as Mary received only stares.

Tina said, "It would take something only a Star Child could do. When Tom opened the Sanctuary

119

door he had to use enhanced vision to look inside and see the inside latch, then he had to use telekinesis to move it. I bet it will be something like that."

Mary said, "You're probably right. I'll try."

Mary focused her enhanced vision on the hatch and began letting her vision focus penetrate the metal, and slowly she began to advance her focus through the metal until she was seeing inside. Yes, she saw the latch and grabbed it with her telekinesis and pulled. There was a rush of air as the hatch began to open. They all moved back, not knowing what direction the hatch would open. It began opening downward a little to their left. A bright light flashed on as the hatch lowered.

Bridget telepathically transmitted, *"Yeah! I see you got it open. Great job you guys. If you are going in now, Colonel Burns wants to go with you if it's all right. One of you want to come get him, or do you want one of us to bring him?"*

"We better keep two of you there in the saucer. You need to monitor the temperature in the tunnel and not let it freeze over behind you. Jerry will come get him." Jerry nodded and floated down, but he was back within minutes holding the colonel within his bubble. Jerry unceremoniously dropped him on the ramp of the open hatch to join the rest of them.

As they walked up the ramp, lighting automatically came on to light their way. It became apparent that the hatch opened up in the center of the bottom of the ship, and the circular design clearly indicated they were inside a very large

120

saucer. Next to the outside ramp stood another ramp leading up to the next level. This ramp was obviously also retractable and appeared to perfectly match and seal to the opening in the floor above.

Colonel Burns said, "Damn, this saucer is huge."

Gary said, "From our research we know that we are in the propulsion and engineering level, which is one of the smallest levels. Just wait till you see the rest of the ship, if you think this is huge." All the kids were watching the colonel's reaction and smiling.

The colonel said, "After, what, over 900 years, how can there still be power for lighting and operations? I feel the air moving and it's not freezing in here, so there must still be power."

Mary said, "ARC generates its own power, like the Sanctuary. You wouldn't believe me if I told you how much power ARC is capable of producing. The problem with ARC was not with a loss of power. It was the fact that no one was here to tell it what to do, and it went dormant, except for basic operations. When we entered, it activated. Now we must go to the control room and give it instructions."

They proceeded up the next ramp into level two, which Colonel Burns could recognize nothing. What he did notice was the design. Each level so far was completely sealable for environmental control, as also was each pie-shaped radius room extending outward to the perimeter of the ship. Each level presented a somewhat different design and layout for the central most areas. There was no wasted space to be seen but also not cramped.

As they continued their upward journey into level three, he saw layers upon layers of honeycombed compartments facing inward along the entire outside extremity, following the circumference that was visible. He marveled at how immense this level had become.

Mary, seeing his puzzled stare, said, "We are in one of the largest levels. Levels three and four, the next one up, support the saucer's wings, which extend out almost the width of this space all the way around."

Colonel Burns said, "Wow! Just how big is this monster?"

Mary laughed and said, "As we mentioned earlier at the meetings, it's much larger than your largest aircraft carrier, not even counting the wings."

"Now, if you are wondering what the honeycomb structures are, they are cryogenic chambers that would house twenty-five thousand bodies. The Arcadians used them for the long voyage to Earth when they evacuated our dying planet."

Continuing his assessment, he observed that most of the rest of the deck seemed to be medical support and equipment to support the cryogenic process. The kids led and actually pushed him forward up the next ramp into the forth deck level. This deck became recognizable immediately. It could easily be identified as living quarters, mess hall, recreation area, and general living facilities.

He was shocked as they entered the fifth and sixth decks. Both decks were open, meaning that there was no floor between them. The area was wide open and were unmistakably dedicated for use as green houses for food and oxygen generation for long-term life support. Half of the bottom deck was filled with earth with large ponds of water that appeared to circulate in streams, while the upper deck was full of trees. He didn't recognize any of them, but then why would he? They were from another world. Birds, at least he thought they were birds, sang and flew between the trees, and other small animals could be heard chattering. The ecosphere of plants, animals, and other organisms must have been perfectly designed, because there remained a thriving and living forest after so many centuries. He was mesmerized, and the kids laughed at him. He noticed that the kids were not at all surprised that the ecosystem remained intact.

At Colonel Burns questioning look, Mary simply said, "It's automated and was designed to operate in perpetuity."

The Star Children were also in automated mode. They were eager to reach the control room to fully activate the ship, so they lowered the ramp leading up into the seventh and top deck, the Master Control Center. Once there, the kids forgot about him and took seats around a console curved partly around the center section seemingly facing the front. He didn't know just how anyone would know what was the front on a perfectly round saucer, but there it was. The Arcadians, in this unearthly setting, seemed more appropriate for them, slipped communications belts around their heads and began letting their fingers flip through lights that magically appeared before them. They began doing what they came here to do.

He then began surveying his surroundings. He suddenly realized that this seventh deck was the extreme top of the ship, and it consisted of a huge dome of transparent material. Initially he hadn't noticed that fact, because of the ice covering it. Surrounding the center consul in ever widening circles were swivel chairs fastened to the deck. His assumption was that this area functioned as a large auditorium, large conference room, or observation deck.

After a few moments Mary said, "ARC is now active, and we have started the hull heating process. We should soon begin slowly sinking through the ice, but the process could take days, possibly even longer, to melt out the bottom. I have also notified Sue of our status to report to the committee. Tina, Jerry, and I will remain onboard to continue checking out all the operational systems, but it looks good so far. I suggest you go back with Gary and Don and report what you have seen here. I think you might have a lot so say." Colonel Burns just smiled.

Chapter 7
(The Plan)

The daily archive meetings had ceased for the last week, except for the individual teams. The military delegation had decided that they needed to be seen back at their commands, so there would be no suspicion. Tom thought that was sensible and gave them a week off. He did, however, provide transportation to a secluded location back in America where they would not be seen with the Star Children. The week had passed and all members were back for the resumption of today's meeting.

Again, Sue wanted to go first. Tom and Sue shared the responsibility of leadership, and he did not begrudge her portion of the leadership duties. Sue said, "The good news is that Mary and Jerry's team have not only found the Mother Ship, but they have accessed it and have begun the melting process to excavate it from the ice shelf. They report that all appears to be operational and the ARC's archive has already linked with the Sanctuary's archive. They have also verified that the satellites we discussed are in inventory. The Mother Ship should be totally functional within days. Colonel Burns, I understand you have actually been onboard ARC. Would you like to comment?"

Colonel Burns, uncharacteristic for him, was grinning hugely and said, "Incredible is the word I would use to describe the experience. The Mother Ship is monstrous in size and abundant in advanced technology. There are seven deck levels of perfectly laid out and efficient structures and stored supplies. They even have an Arcadian forest growing inside, complete with animals, insects, and exotic plant life, even huge trees. It was an unbelievable experience. I was shocked just entering the lower deck. The first surprise I saw was a store of five additional saucers like the ones we have here, plus four satellites stored like we discussed It also has a deck with massive cryogenic storage and medical facilities. I wasn't expecting that. But, the most fascinating deck was the upper deck, the Control Complex. It was mostly open space inside a transparent crystal dome. I witnessed magical monitors and control apparatus appear in the air as needed. It came across as higher tech than Star Wars or any other Sci-Fi move I have ever seen."

"Also however, came the sobering realization that ARC represents the most awesome war machine this world has ever seen. With the weapons I have seen, many of which I don't even understand, they could easily dominate and control Earth if they wished."

General Warner asked, "Should we be worried with the reactivation of the Mother Ship?"

Tom quickly answered, "Only if you try to attack us here. Remember our discussion? We decided to find and reactivate ARC in the eventuality we needed to defend ourselves … for helping you, I might add. But, you have no worries from us. The Arcadians were and Star Children are a benevolent race. We have no desire to dominate or control Earth. Our race came to Earth, our new

126

home, to live in peace and to help humanity evolve and develop, which is what we are now doing."

"Sorry. I meant no offense, but thank you for your assurance." Tom dipped his head in response.

Admiral Jones said, "I'm thankful to be able to count on the ARC for our defense. Might I ask if the teleportation devise has been checked out and activated? Will we be able to use it for our planned Coup for certain operations?"

Tom smiled hugely and pointed toward the end of the room, where the air was already shimmering. The intensity grew and instantly Tina flashed into existence. All, except the Star Children, having been forewarned, jumped to their feet in astonishment.

Tina said, "I wanted to be the first to fly like this." The Star Children laughed, knowing Tina's love of flying. After a moment she began shimmering again and disappeared.

Tom said, "Does that answer your question, admiral?" There was no need to wait for an answer and continued, "Sorry for the dramatics, the Star Children follow these meeting remotely, and Mary thought this surprise might come in handy in answering your anticipated question, while providing a little humor. From all your reactions I would say that it worked."

Admiral Jones said, "It did indeed."

Tom said, "Berta, would you like to report on your team's progress?"

Berta was still laughing as she took the podium and said, "Well, we have identified the mind control signal and designed a method of modulating the signal into the beginning sequence of every audio transmission to ensure its secrecy. We tried the audio transmission out on general Barney. Does it work, general?"

General Barney of the NSA struggled to speak about the phone message, but he could say nothing, even though he tried. All he was able to say was, "Yes."

General Warner bellowed, "I don't like you messing with the military delegation with your mind control!"

Dr. Wisscroff stood and said, "I am the one that suggested this, and I believe all involved in the Coup back in America, including you here should be indoctrinated with the same security restrictions in the same way. Let me tell you why. It only takes one corrupted agent plant … just one, to destroy our security and leak information that will wreck our plans."

"But we came to you for help. We are committed and absolutely secure."

Dr. Wisscroff said, "Hummm Really? There was a reason we chose General Barney. Berta, would you like to address this subject?"

Berta said, "I would be happy too. Our vetting of patriot members has been ongoing since the last meeting, and it is producing many interesting facts. The military delegation of leaders, both here and back in America has not been excluded. Our archive sees everything present and past, and it operates incredibly fast, especially since the two archives have linked. I told you nothing is exempt from our hacks. Oh let me not drag this out. General Warner, did you know you are soon to be replaced as the Chairman of the Joint Chief of Staff?" The general's eyes visibly bugged. "Maybe you might want to congratulate your replacement, General Barney." General Warner shot a hard stare at General Barney. "There was a reason we picked General Barney to start with. We monitored his encrypted communications with the president." When an angry General Barney jumped to his feet, he was slammed back down in his seat by Colonel Burns, who had been warned.

"There are many ways to bribe someone, even without money; and promotion is one of the biggest ways. Luckily, they are still in negotiations, so he wouldn't have shown his hand yet and hasn't revealed any of our plans that we know of. But, it's only a matter of time. Fortunately he can't leak those plans now, and he hasn't anything to negotiate with now. I guess that means you keep your job, General Warner."

General Bruner said, "The bastard is a fucking traitor and should be shot!"

Tom said, "Well, that is a decision for the military delegation.".

General Warner looked hard at General Barney and said, "We will take that under advisement, general."

Dr. Wisscroff said, "See what I mean by absolute security being a necessity. This is why everyone involved in this coup receive the audio control. Remember, it only takes one leak to destroy our whole plan." General Warner's forlorn expression and nod conveyed that he agreed.

Berta had remained at the podium during the exchanges, now continued, "Like I was saying earlier, our vetting process is going well. Already we have identified many potential moles and eliminated them from the membership list, but we have cleared over two million dedicated and committed patriots. We are scanning all the social media venues to find more. If they are pissed enough to make an angry post, we will pull them into the network. We don't want them acting alone without our direction. We figure the calm before will increase the shock of the storm. Our current estimate should reach over five million, maybe many more. We will just have to see."

"The Hit List seems to be growing. Some are suggesting we add additional targets of terror cells, unions leaders, major criminals, violent psychopaths, anarchist group leaders, etc. I've talked to General Bruner and he assures me that many of those are already in the list, especially union leaders and anarchist groups. He says they are part of the 50,000 in the Misc. list. But, adding additional targets will expand the list. What is the committee's opinion on this?"

Dr. Wisscroff said, "This is a gift, this Coup. It's our opportunity to do a major sweep of the bad guys. I mean, we have already decided to assassinate over a half a million souls. What's a few more? Terror cells are planning to kill as many Americans as they can. Violent psychopaths are the serial killers doing the same thing. Major criminals are killing and robbing innocent people. I would say they have earned a slot on the list."

No one else spoke up, so after a long pause Berta said, "I guess that question has been answered"

"The next phase we have been analyzing are the targets for the funding. We have identified almost fifty-billion we can seize." Many expletives were echoed.

Admiral Jones said, "Damn! That's a lot of money. Where are you getting it from and what are you going to do with the money?"

"Well, mostly we just want to take it away from the Communist funders so it can't be used by the operatives to continue their assault or for their defense. Without money they have no power and can do nothing. Mostly we have targeted those we mentioned earlier. Specifically, we identified one extremely wealthy, globalist billionaire that seems to have his hands in many of the subversive, Communist organizations and funds them heavily."

"This industrialist has been active in numerous funding and bribing campaigns to insert his own operatives into high government positions. He has corrupted many of the states Attorney Generals, Secretary of State positions, and some governors in order to steal the last presidential election in swing states. He is a heavy player and is personally worth about ten billion. We calculate we can seize about six billion of his net worth after we sell off his stocks without his knowledge. Since he is a major player on the wrong side, we plan to disrupt his companies and investments to cost him several more billion. He will no longer be a player or funder for a very long time, assuming he even survives his reserved place on the Hit List."

"We are targeting several more billionaires as well, but these are not as bad as the one we hope to destroy. We'll just take their money. Additionally, we target some major corporations lobbying for socialist laws in Congress. We are taking funds from many of the Democrat fund raising PACs and a couple of Republican's as well. It kind of depends on who they have contributed to in the past. If they have supported those that are subversive, they lose their funds."

"Some of our major targets are the social media companies. They have done massive damage to America by corrupting and spreading their subversive ideology and attacking those trying to help America. Some on the Hit List targets are the wealthy owners and key executives. We intend to take much of their wealth and destroy the companies by transferring some of the money into many of the other corrupt activists' accounts. Any forensic audit will be able to easily identify the transfer of funds, thanks to the footprints we will leave, the source and recipient. By doing this we will create targets for any internal investigation and create chaos within the organization."

Berta laughed and continued, "Our team has created a strategy of using unsuspecting sources as our assassins by taking funds from terrorist organizations and Mexican cartels and transferring traceable, token amounts into corrupt politician and bureaucrats in the NSA, DOJ, FBI, and others' accounts. Again we will leave a digital trail to ensure the targets will be easily identified. Given the nature of the funding sources, the targets will be found and assuredly eliminated without our involvement other than the seizing of their funds."

"We plan to initiate this plan on some before the Coup as a trial run and launch. Any initial assassinations can be traced back to the terrorist and cartels that will focus any investigation on a false trail, ahead of the main Coup."

General Bruner said, "Damn, girl, I like the way you think." He looked at Tom and the rest of the Star Children and said, "I thought Mr. Mum said Arcadians and Star Children are not noted for their clever subterfuge and manipulation. This certainly paints a different picture."

Tom said, "Mr. Mum also said that we are always focused toward helping humanity. That is exactly what we are doing. Yes, we are intelligent and can plan and calculate strategies, and Berta is doing just that, quite well I might add."

Berta continued, "We are even planning on taking some funds from the United Nations' hidden in secret accounts that funds subversive activities. We're going to take funds from corrupt politicians where we have identified the source as bribes and kickbacks. Some of these corrupt, career politicians have become very wealthy through kickbacks and bribes. Should I go on?"

After no one spoke, Tom said, "I think we all get the idea, but Admiral Jones asked a second question about where we plan to put the money. You might address that question."

Berta said, "When we take the funds from an account we scrub the account records of any transfer data. It just disappears, but we have to put it somewhere when we take it. When I asked Dr. Wisscroff where the money should go, he suggested to put it back in America's Social Security fund that Congress stole, or pay it toward the national debt. So, we have created a method to do both. Do you have suggestions of other areas we could put the funds?"

General Warner said, "Actually, those are good locations. I would normally suggest funds applied to the military budget, but until the Coup is complete those funds could be used poorly. I might suggest that funds mysteriously appear in the 'Complete the Wall' Texas budget, since our current idiot president cut off the funds. It would also be nice to have some funds assigned to us to help launch this Coup effort. We are operating with no budget or funds."

Tom said, "The problem is that we can't seize the funds until closer to the day of the Coup or they will be forewarned. We here, the Sanctuary, have abundant funds, which we can help you with immediately. We can fund the wall on the day of the Coup. Just let Berta know what you need and she is authorized to dispense a reasonable amount of funds to a secure, untraceable account she sets up. Is that satisfactory?" The general nodded enthusiastically, along with the others in the delegation.

Admiral Jones said, "I'm curious how you gathered your abundant funds. Have you previously seized funds and that's how you know it will work?

I'm not criticizing if you have. I don't care where the funds came from. I'm just curious."

Tom grinned and said, "No, we haven't seized any funds. We have actually earned it the old fashioned way. We earned it honestly. Dr. Wisscroff has filed certain patents for us. We are a corporation under the name of The Sanctuary. Dr. Wisscroff filed patents for some of the technology we deem safe to release to the world. Just wait until our antigravity cars hit the market. All the automobile companies are buying into our patents, and we are making a fortune from the royalties. The cars also have their own power generator, another patent, and the car will never need gas. Well, they aren't really cars, since they don't roll or even touch the roads, but their elevation will be restricted, so they will have to follow the existing highway system. I hope that satisfies your curiosity." The general grinned and nodded.

During the momentary silence between subjects General Bruner blurted out, "What is going to be done about the traitor?" Silence filled the room.

It was an Air Force general that spoke. General Smith said, "If he is unable to reveal anything about our plans, maybe we could use him for our purposes. He has been a patriot up to this point. I mean he did help organize this delegation and plan a Coup, so hopefully he still is a patriot at heart and just had a weak moment. If not, we can always add him to the Hit List or follow General Bruner's suggestion. He now knows we can reach him and this is not an idle threat. It might benefit us to send him back and have a man on the inside of the NSA to steer them in the wrong direction, so they don't look here. Russia or China would be good choices. Could you do that General Barney?"

General Barney, eager to find an out of his treachery, jumped to his feet and said, "Yes ... yes, I can send them so far off course they will never find their way back. Just give me the chance."

General Warner said, "That might be a great idea as long as we can be assured he will comply. Is there any way to monitor him?"

General Bruner said, "Yes there is. John, we still have a supply of the implants we used in what you called the Alien War. Once you launch the satellites, we could monitor him through the implant and detonate it if he tries to renege."

John looked at Tom and said, "Normally I would not want to go that far. As you recall, I had one of those implants, and I hated the implants when we had to deal with them before, but in this case I tend to agree. We can't take a chance."

Tom said, "Berta, are you able to monitor those implants through the archive?"

She said, "Yes."

"General Barney, are you willing to take the implant considering the alternative?"

He said, "Yes."

"Anyone opposed?" None spoke. "So be it."

**

Mary, Jerry, and Tina had spent two days nursing and checking out the ARC. As with all the technology the Arcadians had invented and built, they found everything working and in top condition. They had even operated the teleport during the last

136

meeting. Tina insisted. They had been monitoring the meeting and Tina ran down the ramp saying for us to teleport her into the meeting. They did and it was incredibly dramatic and at the perfect time. Tina was giggling when she came back to the control room.

Mary asked, "What did it feel like? Were you scared?

"No, I wasn't scared at all. It just tingled and then I was there. I liked it, but it scared the crap out of the humans there."

They had been experimenting with the teleport for the better part of a day, learning how to monitor and adjust the focus or target area. They could actually see the target area on the monitor and the surrounding people and objects. All they had to do was place an X on the target or an X on the destination and flick the blue indicator to transmit or receive the flick the activate red light. Searching for the destination target area was a little more complicated. Jerry had mentioned that it was almost like using Google Earth. You started out with an Earth view, then kept clicking and expanding until you had your target, even through structures. They were already focused on the conference room when Tina got her sudden inspiration, so it wasn't difficult to comply. It did come as a surprise, however.

They were still laughing at the reaction it caused when an alarm sounded, indicating that the ship was beginning to slip out of its icy prison. Jerry went to the controls and monitor to view the digital image of the ice and the ship within it. He saw that the ship was mostly already clear of the ice. Just a few shards of ice remained to hold it.

Jerry said, "I don't think we need to wait any longer. We can break out easy enough without any damage."

Mary said, "Great. Do it."

Jerry nudged the controls and rocked the ship back and forth gently and watched the remaining ice break away. They were free. Jerry lowered the ARC down then forward through the water. His confidence grew and he speeded up and zoomed through the water, but he quickly backed off when he felt the massive turbulence created by the huge ship pushing an incredible volume of water as it pushed through.

Jerry said, "Mary, you might want to notify Tom and the others to come up on the ice shelf to see the marvel of the ARC. See if they want a tour. I can set it down by the entrance, but they might want to see it land." She nodded.

Jerry took his time traveling under the ice shelf and according to the digital monitor they finally cleared the ice shelf and emerged from the water into open air. At that point Jerry shot up high in the air and kept going straight into the vacuum of space.

Mary said, "Where are you going, the moon?"

"Well, we could. It wouldn't take us that long, but I just wanted to get a feel of the ship. We have a little time before they can get outside."

But all those inside must have scrambled, because Tom was already asking where they were. They wanted them to see the wonder of ARC, so they turned off the invisibility stealth and quickly returned to the entrance to the Sanctuary. They came in slow and settled down near the Marine camp. When they lowered the bottom ramp, the entire group from the conference room came bounding inside. Tina was waiting for them when they entered.

***

The meeting was in full swing, but Sue jumped up and interrupted whoever was speaking and shouted, "The ARC is free and is en route to the outside entrance if anyone wants to see it."

All the attendees jumped up also and mass exited for the entrance. They were not going to miss this historic event.

Sue quickly said, "If you are not a Star Child be sure to grab your coats. It's 20 below outside!"

Colonel Burns led the group up on the elevator in groups, and they gathered on a snow bank so they could watch the event. The visibility was adequate, even though the sun was low on the horizon. As they watched, a massive object blotted out the sun. The object took shape of an immense flying saucer far bigger than they expected. He had toured the ship from the inside, but seeing it from the outside was a completely difference experience. The shape appeared to be a perfectly round fried egg … a really big fried egg. It looked identical to the fighter craft the Star Children flew, but much, much bigger. In the center ball section the height looked to be fifteen stories, even along the outside edge it had to be a couple of stories tall. The color was bright, pinkish silver; well, actually almost translucent, but not quite, just like the smaller ones. ARC slowly

139

settled lower, support struts opened on the bottom, and as it settled to rest on the ice, a ramp opened in the bottom of the egg. Tina was standing there waving and beckoning them to enter.

The colonel led the group quickly up the ramp and into the warmth of the ship, pointing out the parts he had learned on his original tour. Tina corrected him only a few times. The Star Children in the group were seeing and learning as well, since they had not downloaded any of the archive data.

Berta said, "Tina, can you show us the teleport? I would love to see it, and I think the others would like to see it, also."

Tina said, "Sure. It's on the second deck. Follow me."

Tina led them up the ramp into the second deck and down a corridor into a room housing large, glass tubes, which were abundantly large enough for two humans inside. The tubes appeared to be about seven feet tall and resting on a short, circular pedestal. As Tina walked toward one, it split open to allow her to walk inside. When she entered, the glass closed around her. She smiled and moved forward again, and the glass reopened.

Tina said, "It's operated from the control room, which you will see last."

The group marveled at the strange and complex equipment as they continued up through each deck. Colonel Burns offered some narration as they went, but none was offered in the 5th and 6th. The majesty of the Arcadian forest spoke for itself. As they traversed the last ramp and entered the Control Room, all stopped to take in the awesome wonder of the room. The huge, crystal dome and view outside added to the experience.

Mary and Jerry sat at the controls, and Mary said, "Welcome to the ARC. Would you like to take a victory ride with us?" No one said anything, but the nodding heads answered.

Jerry smiled, because he had already planned a surprise, and said, "This ship utilizes artificial gravity, so there will be no need to strap in. You can stand or sit … no matter. You will feel no inertia from our acceleration and the deck will always be down, even if we fly upside down. I have a short trip planned. Here we go."

The ship instantly shot up in the air and zoomed off toward space. The only way they could tell was by watching the blurred movement outside the crystal dome. They were soon deep in space and Jerry rolled the ship to watch Earth shrink as they went higher. Jerry then righted the ship and the moon began to get larger by the second. Once all in the viewing area had a solid reference as to where they were, Jerry shot forward at an incredible speed. Almost instantly they were orbiting the moon. The ship completed the moon orbit and shot back to Earth to begin a slow orbit. Needless to say, all were shocked and most took seats to steady their shaking legs.

Surprisingly, it was Tom that said, "Damn! That was impressive." After a moment of thought he asked, "Are we in stealth mode?"

Mary said, "Absolutely. We have been invisible since we took off. Radar nor eyesight can detect us. What do you think, Dr. Wisscroff?"

"Incredible! I've been an astrophysics for over fifty years, and this is the first time I've left Earth. I want to be a regular fixture on the ARC when it explores space, like I know we will eventually do."

Sue said, "Maybe someday, Dr. Wisscroff, but right now we need you at the Sanctuary."

Dr. Wisscroff frowned but said, "Very well. I understand."

Mary said, "Unless you have pressing questions that can't wait, we need to get back to business. We have already activated three of the satellites and they are functioning perfectly. We will drop you all back at the Sanctuary, but we thought you might like to see the ARC before we begin launching the satellites."

Berta said, "Are you going to space them at 120 degrees to have total world coverage should we need it?"

"Absolutely! We haven't discussed it, but you should all know that these satellites have their own power generating source and gravity-drive, so they can be repositioned as might be needed. It has sufficient self-power to more than support its own built in laser and stealth. It's also capable of many other function in communications as we have discussed, but it's also capable of self-defense or used as an offensive weapon."

Berta said, "I would like to go, if you can bring me back to the Sanctuary afterwards."

Dr. Wisscroff said, "Me too!"

Mary said, "Sure, we can do that, or we can teleport you directly back into the Sanctuary if you like. Would any of you like to try out the teleport

142

now?" No one volunteered. "No takers? Tina says it's fun. That's alright, we will pick up Don, Gary, Karen, and Bridget when we let you out. They are waiting to help us launch the satellites."

As they settled to the snow, many from the Sanctuary and the Marine detachment had gathered outside in the cold to see the ARC. They cheered as the ramp lowered. Most disembarked as the rest of the ARC team entered. Jerry didn't wait long before he rose several hundred feet and shot out and up toward the magical geostationary orbit heights of 22,236 miles. Of course it's not magical at all, it is simple math. At this calculated distance from Earth the satellite orbits at the same speed the Earth turns and an object positioned there will remain stationary in reference to a position on Earth.

Once they reached the orbit altitude, Jerry turned the artificial gravity off on the lower deck, making the large satellites weightless. The three satellites were then positioned near the bottom ramp to await maneuvering to the calculated three coordinates. Don and Gary formed their personal air and pressure bubbles and evacuated the air from the deck. Each satellite was pushed out at the proper point and the deck repressurized with air. At that point the job was complete.

Chapter 8
(Test Plan)

Berta spoke first at today's meeting. "You will probably find this interesting, but with Tom and Sue's approval, we ran a preliminary test of our Coup hack to see how it would go. The results of the first hack and seizure of funds came off flawless, like we knew it would. We chose as the target the Denton Foundation, which was first on General Bruner's list of the worst offenders. As all of you know, there have been many investigations launched against the Dentons and a great deal of evidence of foul play has been exposed. But, have any of you seen *any* indictments or conviction? They all seem to fizzle out, and then we hear no more about it. They are neck deep in the corruption syndicate and are protected by the corrupted DOJ and FBI. The Denton Foundation, as we all know, was the receiver of bribery and pay off funds for the Pay-for-Play scheme Secretary of State, Halley Denton, set up during a previous administration. The tax-free foundation took in many millions of dollars from countries and wealthy individuals and corporations around the world, who seemed to mysteriously receive favors for their contributions."

"This was also a test to get confirmation from the corrupt operatives. Not only did we confirm many of the bad players, but our actions ultimately eliminated some of them. Some have now been removed from our Hit List. By that I mean they met with mysterious deaths, which is not so uncommon for those that threaten the Dentons or the Denton Foundation. The suspected known deaths attributed to the Dentons is in the hundreds."

"Our team seized funds from the Denton Foundation leaving a false data trail, which we created, to a few of the politicians associated with the Dentons on our Hit List. We also routed the funds through one of the corrupt directors at the NSA. All the corrupt players know that you don't mess with the Dentons and live to talk about it. We couldn't provide a large list of targets. That would be too suspicious, but we put ten million into two of the corrupt, senior Senators' bank accounts and routed the whole transaction through a high level operative at the NSA to create an apparent conspiracy. A sum that large would certainly be noticed. It obviously was, because within two days the two Senators were dead and the NSA director disappeared. One Senator died of a sudden heart attack and the other died in a car accident the next day. The NSA director is probably six feet under somewhere or in the foundation of a newly constructed building in D.C."

"We provided an anonymous and untraceable leak to the media that the Denton Foundation had been hacked and money taken, and we even told them who received the funds. We wanted to see who would run with the story and how the Denton's would react. The reaction was predictable, CNN, MSNBC, and the alphabet network news said nothing. They didn't even mention it at all. FOX, NEWSMAX, and a few of the smaller independent news outlets did carry the story and reported that the Dentons claimed it was a total hoax, and that all their funds were still intact. They were careful not to use the words 'Fake News'. Some of those that ran the story are starting to question the mysterious deaths of the Senators, whose names we leaked to them prior, but the connection has gotten no traction and probably won't. The Denton's money still remains in the Senator's accounts, so they are obviously afraid to go after it at this time, but our test has severely harmed their funding ability and set them back for a long time."

"The test worked out perfectly, and the satellite network is now up and operational and will drastically improve our capabilities. We are now ready for the funds seizure phase of our plan."

General Warner said, "I have a question concerning another part of the plan. I fully understand the subliminal security message requirement, but we have been wondering what exactly we are going to say in audible words in this initial message and what we hope to accomplish. Should we discuss the content?"

Tom said, "That's a good question. Who wants to respond?"

Fred said, "I have been working on that part, the technology anyway. Once we developed the, as General Warner calls it, subliminal signal, we felt relatively sure of the security, but we decided to keep that same signal on during any exchange and throughout the entire communication process. That way the phone can't be given over to another that

146

bypasses the embedded command. The command will be constantly generated."

"We plan to establish a remote phone number/s, totally secure and encrypted then routed through our own satellite network. It will be impossible for any entity to track or decode any communication on our network. Now, before I go on, I need to explain our vetting process. We, through our extremely fast archive and faster exponentially with the activation of ARC, which you would probably relate to as a supercomputer, have processed vast amounts of information on each person listed in your contact lists we hacked. We know everything about them and have located and analyzed every social media posts they ever made to verify their commitment. We know their mindset and that they are real patriots before we allow them to remain active in our database. These members are identified by each of their cell phone numbers. Those numbers are their member IDs, along with a code number that they must provide when we call. These instructions will be provided in their subliminal commands. We will also be able to voice identify them. Actually, we have their voice codes already recorded. We believe we have a very secure process in place."

"The plan as we envision it is to call each member that has passed the vetting process and verify their desires. We believe we should be honest with them up front about the pending Coup, the necessity and manner of our security measures, seek their level of intended involvement, and … I'm sure we can add other information we can pass on. They should know many of the details, since they will be

147

unable to talk about it due to the subliminal commands. They want to be involved, and we want them to be committed. So, they should be able to know what's involved. We have read many of the messages they have sent to the generals and admirals here and those back in America, plus their social media posts. We have also hacked and reviewed many of the politicians' constituents communications archives to identify a great number of potential members. They want and demand a Coup, and like Admiral Jones pointed out previously, if we don't guide them they will act on their own. So, they need to be informed and involved. I might add, there are millions of them."

"By the way, have we sat a date for the Coup? We believe it critical to make contact with the membership soon to prevent unwanted action from them. I believe we are ready, but we need to establish a timeline and target date before we can actually begin the contacts. Plus, we need time to coordinate the targets and hit teams." Fred waited for an answer.

Tom said, "Are we all ready? Maybe I should ask, is anyone *not* ready?" No one responded.

"Well, can we agree and schedule the Coup for one month from today?" Again, no one responded. "Very well, let's schedule the coup for Dec. 7, to match another date in America's history that lives in infamy."

Berta said, "That's too soon. We need more time to implement the plan. Let's give it another month. Can we make it Jan. … 6? Isn't that the date of the falsely claimed coup?" All around the table laughed at the irony.

"Now you have a date, Fred."

General Warner said, "We need to get General Barney equipped with the implant and back in the NSA. I don't think the current president will replace him now, since he thinks he has switched sides. We need him on the inside to steer any future investigation in the wrong direction." General Barney nodded like he was back in the fold, which he probably was … with limitations and renewed motivation.

John said, "We can take care of that and deliver him back to DC secretly."

The ever thoughtful Dr. Wisscroff said, "There is more that needs to be done. The average citizens of America needs to support the Coup openly after it happens. Mrs. Wilks was correct when she brought it up before, but the timing wasn't right. But, I think the timing is right now. There needs to be marches organized and rallies in support of the Coup. But, all the citizens of the US needs to know what happened and why and that it wasn't a terrorist attack. We aren't taking out all the bad players, and they need to be warned to change their ways. In lack of a story, the media *will* come up with their own story, so let's give them one … the right one. We should write up a story, no, a manifesto for America."

General Toma said, "That's an excellent idea! It will inform the citizens not yet knowledgeable or involved, guide the new government, and focus the media. Not only that, a manifesto should define the demands of the Coup, something we haven't really discussed."

Tom said, "I totally agree. Dr. Wisscroff I think you just volunteered to write the American Manifesto. You know better than anyone what has gone wrong with the government, you know who the enemy is, and you know what needs to be done and the direction America should move toward. Maybe you can get with the military delegation for help. They have firsthand knowledge of what needs to happen. Us kids haven't been around long enough to even have thoughts about it. We are doing this for defense, and to help humanity. We won't be living in your world."

Dr. Wisscroff gave one of his rare smiles and said, "Yes, I am probably the one that could best write the manifesto, and of course Mrs. Wilks should be involved. She has lived in America, well not quite as long as I but long enough to have some strong opinions. But we will definitely seek help and ideas from these learned gentlemen." Mrs. Wilks smiled and nodded her approval.

After a few days the daily meetings were becoming unproductive, so Tom began limiting them to only one day per week. The rest of the time the members separated into working groups in various categories and work progressed much faster.

It had been two weeks since the last full committee meeting and General Toma went first to report the progress of his group, recruitment. General Toma said, "Good morning. It has been a very productive two weeks since the last meeting, and we have made significant progress. I can report over twenty-million recruits have joined our ranks, and six million of those are committed and trained, trigger soldiers. The numbers could easily be a much larger member group, but keep in mind that with the subliminal silence command, word of mouth doesn't occur. All these members have come onboard by us contacting them, and we are being cautiously selective. " The general stopped to let those number register in their minds.

Dr. Wisscroff, totally uncharacteristic for him as an intellectual, blurted out, "No shit! Really? That's an incredible number. How in the world are you keeping the process secure?"

General Toma laughed and said, "Yes, shit! Being isolated here in the Sanctuary, you probably missed the election fraud where President Thompson lost the fraudulent and stolen election. Amazing, since he got the highest vote for president in history, over 75 million … except this idiot president got more … Really? Well, I guess that should be expected since every dead person for the last 100 years seemed to come alive and vote on the idiot check mark, plus the corrupted Democrats and their henchmen managed to control the entire election process to ensure President Dufus got elected. The sudden conversion by corrupt and controlled officials to computer voting virtually ensured that they could manipulate and control the numbers. I'm telling you, the population at large is pissed off and willing to do anything in protest and reverse that lie of an election."

"So damn much evidence has been exposed, even videos of election workers running ballots in the middle of the night and multiple times, but the compromised DOJ and FBI refuse to investigate and the judges refuse to take the lawsuits filed. This entire election scam has pissed off virtually every patriot in America, and I mean really, really pissed them off. We the people have lost control of our government, and the patriots know it. The Communist have taken control. As a result, we could probably get an incredible number of members, but the risk of exposure does increase with higher numbers. The risk is minimal but continues to bear watching."

"You asked how we are maintaining security. We maintain it by being absolutely sure of who we contact. Berta has already talked about the background checks that are verified front and back. We know virtually everything about a potential member. Still, we approach them carefully with a BOT (automated computer robot) call from our secure and isolated phone lines that simply asks a question: **Do you support the revolution that is coming? If so, and you want to be involved, call us back at this number.** Of course the initial call provides the subliminal command to remain silent. When they return the call on that number, and most of them do, the archive confirms their identity and provides a second BOT message detailing our Coup plan, like has been discussed. We give the members a choice as to the level of involvement they will commit to: **(1) Support the Coup by marches, rallies, protests - (2) Defend against anarchist and government officials' resistance - (3)**

Participate as a soldier in the Coup - (4) High level involvement to remove corrupt operatives."

"As you can see each level increases the level of commitment. The added benefit is that it lets the member know what to expect. Virtually, all potential members, at a minimum, commit to at least the first category. Many of these are older veterans and would have a hard time stepping up to the higher level, but surprising, or not so surprising, we have a large number committing to the forth category and want to be a soldier in the Coup. And, like I've said, six million have stepped up to be triggers. This is far more than we need, so some will be assigned to protect the marches, rallies, and protests, and when I say protect, I mean take out those that try to attack or disrupt these gatherings, especially the anarchist groups."

"Each member of each category is thoroughly indoctrinated in what is expected of them, and they are enthusiastically dedicated to the task. The first three groups will come into play on the day after the initial coup to show support for the Coup and the American Manifesto. Obviously, the fourth group will activate on the day and previous night of Dec. 6th."

General Warner stood and said, "All these groups are in addition to the active military which we command. We will mobilize our forces and lock down Congress, the Pentagon if required, the White House, DOJ, FBI, CIA, the Supreme Court, and many other agencies. DC will be totally locked down. We will arrest the president and his staff and remove them from our government. At the same

153

time, we will escort President Thompson back into the White House to resume command of the government and restore his staff. We will recommend and expect President Thompson will declare a state of emergency and temporary Martial Law, but the military leaders will swear our loyalty to President Thompson, so the world will know this is not just a military Coup. It's simply a necessary change of administration to correct a corrupted election. "

Mrs. Wilks said, "Do you expect an armed conflict in accomplishing these things? Also, is President Thompson aware of our activity?"

"No, President Thompson is not aware of any of this. We have purposely kept him and his main advisors out of any of our plans. He has no idea. We want him and his staff to have plausible deniability with the citizens. He can't be publicly associated with the Coup."

"As far as the potential for armed conflict, there is always that risk. But, once the corrupt players have been eliminated from the military, we anticipate total control. Plus, also keep in mind that category three, soldiers of the Coup, number around ten million; and they are dispersed in every segment of the population, including Capital Police, police and sheriff departments around the country, law enforcement in general, patriotic FBI, DOJ, Secret Service agents, and even Congress. The Coup solders exist or will be infiltrated everywhere, and they will be positioned to reinforce the military and smooth the access of the military. There will be our members in virtually every group and segment of the population. Hopefully, there will be no resistance at all."

"Additionally, on the eve of the Coup, we will massively expand the recruitment of members. Any leak at that point will be too late to stop it, and by doing this we hope to have over fifty-million members to support the Coup and Manifesto."

Mrs. Wilks said, "Thank you general for the insight. This whole plan seems incredibly smooth and efficient."

John stood next and said, "Yes, a massive amount of planning has gone into this Coup, and we have built many safeguards into it. General Bruner and I have also come to an understanding. In regard to Sue's earlier suggestion of transferring the to the Underworld some of those targeted as opposed to assassination. We have agreed that the Underworld will accept up to 25,000 immigrants to relocate to the Underworld, but we can and must be selective with the choices. That is only a small percentage of what Sue had in mind, but that is the amount the Underworld feels they can support. Still, the alternative is death."

"We are interested in accepting engineers and professionals, but we also need farmers and factory workers as well. They must be under 35 years old and healthy, and you might have a hard time understanding this, they must also be under six feet tall." At the anticipated surprise John laughed and continued. "Understand this, we plan to use the ARC to find and teleport them onboard. Now 25,000 is a lot to process at a critical time of the operation. We will have plenty of General Bruner's'

155

guards, but that's far too many hostiles to control. We plan to manage this by using some of the Star Children to put them into cryogenics until we have the time to safely process them into life in the Underworld. This is also the maximum number of cryogenic chambers available, which also sets the number of immigrants."

"This is the problem that requires them to be under six feet tall. The Arcadians were not tall, most being five feet or less. When they built the cryogenic chambers for their own use, the maximum space allowed was six feet. That sets our limitations."

"We have come to some additional agreements, but I will let the general report on them. General Bruner will you tell the committee what you have come up with?"

"Earlier in these meeting I mentioned that the NAZI's Fourth Reich had hidden cells established in America. I have been able to find and activate twenty-five cells. They are four-man teams of trained special forces to take out targets. Most of these are positioned in and around the D.C., L.A., and Dallas areas and can be used to take out the more difficult and protected targets. We estimate that they can take out two hundred, maybe more, of the hardest target in twenty-four hours. We have already assigned them targets and they are preparing as we speak."

"These cells have not been brought in as members of the Coup, because some of them are not susceptible to the mind controls. So, they have no information to leak. But they need no external

156

motivation, just instructions. They have been previously implanted and have no way of knowing the implant cannot now be imploded. Actually, they can be now with the deployment of the satellites, but there is no need to tell them. They will do as they are instructed. The cells are operating independently from what we are doing."

"The squad we will use for the guards aboard the ARC are also trained NAZI special forces. John is allowing us to use them, if necessary, to support any of the operatives in the field that might get into trouble. We can teleport our team wherever they might be needed, but only as last resort, because they are highly lethal and kill any perceived enemy in sight."

Colonel Burns stood to get everyone's attention and said, "I've been an officer in the Marines for many years and have seen conditions under combat. I will tell you that I have concerns about this fourth group, the assassins. What we are asking them to do is mortal combat ... kill people. Can they be trusted to comply and actually do it? I have concerns."

General Warner said, "I'm actually glad that you asked that question, colonel. We really didn't dwell on the details of the vetting process. Keep in mind that there are approximately twenty-million combat service veterans, and the six million committed to the fourth category are mostly military veterans or law enforcement that have seen combat and confirmed kills on their records. For the most part, they are highly trained snipers, Special Forces, Rangers, SEALS, SWAT, and other elite ex and active duty combat personnel. There are even a few recruits from our British allies SAS commando members living in America. Again, they all have seen and been in actual combat, and have recorded kills. This is not their first rodeo, and they know what they are volunteering for and are eager for the opportunity. We have the utmost confidence in these soldiers and are more than comfortable that they will get the job done."

Colonel Burns said, "I'm also glad that I asked that question, because your explanation more than satisfied my concern." General Warner nodded his appreciation.

Chapter 9
(Manifesto)

At today's meeting Dr. Wisscroff was on the agenda to discuss his plans for the Manifesto. The word had gotten out and the conference room was brimming full to hear his lecture, like they all knew it would be.

Dr. Wisscroff took his place at the podium and said, "It's been a long time since I have addressed so many eager to hear my wisdom, but I think I will attribute this large audience size to the subject matter and not the spokesman."

"Mrs. Wilks has helped me analyze and understand the data that must be presented to the entire populations and every facet within. The manifesto must explain what happened to whom, by who, and why, to the other patriots and solicit their support in the days after the Coup. It must provide a strong warning to the remaining corrupt among the populist to conform to a pro America agenda. And, also most important, the manifesto must make demands that must be adhered to. Needless to say, this has been a daunting task."

"I must say that living in the tranquility of the Sanctuary for the last two years has kept me isolated from the activities of the American government. Even before coming here I must have had my head deep in scholarly endeavors, because I had no idea things had gotten as bad as they apparently are. Working with this learned, military delegation has educated me and Mrs. Wilks in the horrors and insanity that has taken place. These generals and admirals have been on the front line of the political battle and up close to all the government corruption and are extremely knowledgeable. It is no wonder they want a Coup."

"Most of the American Manifesto is self-explaining, so I will concentrate on the demands presented, based upon all the information I have gleaned from these gentlemen and lady. These are the following demands:"

"First and foremost, We want a general **Amnesty** provided for the Coup participants. This demand and the others detailed in the American Manifesto are not negotiable, they are mandatory requirements."

"The next important demand we want is the **immediate election decertification** of the last fake election, at a minimum in the swing states; **President Thompson reinstalled;** and immediately conduct new elections as necessary for all down ballots that are in question."

"In the near future before the next election we want verifiable fair and honest elections by **eliminating voting machines** and going back to **paper ballots** that can't be corrupted or hacked. We demand **mandatory Voter ID**, and investigation and **prosecution of voter fraud.**"

"We require a **'Free Press'** The citizens don't want propaganda, they want unbiased reporting and will demand it. We want the news media to be held **liable for Fake News**. They better be prepared to prove their claims in court before they are printed or aired."

"We want **big tech monopolies broken up and controlled** and also held liable. The citizens all saw the biased corruption of the social media companies prior to and after the last election. There is really no need to dwell on the details, since we all saw it. It was shameful and totally one sided politically."

"We want our borders controlled, **immigration laws enforced,** and **finish the border wall**. We were almost there with President Thompson, but that movement came to a crashing halt with the corrupted election of President Dufus. The poor man has no idea what he is doing, he's just following Communist instruction."

"We demand that **anarchist groups be declared domestic terrorist** and prosecuted, those organizations sponsoring and individual rioters that burn, loot, attack police, or act to defund the police. Only the ignorant, insane, or subversives would want to eliminate the police. Anarchy would sweep across the country, which is precisely what they want."

"We demand **protection of the 2nd Amendment.** Our founding fathers specifically added this amendment so the citizens would always have weapons to fight back against a tyrannical government. It seems now that the tyrannical government and its operatives want to confiscate the citizen's weapons. This anti-gun movement is incredibly obvious to the average person, and we want it ended."

161

"**Restore the Constitution** as our sole governing document and impeach any judge that tries to legislate from the bench. In the future, the judicial system will be required to police its own, or the citizens will police it for them with a second wave. I don't think they would want that. The entire judicial system must come back to serving justice."

"Reestablish a **House Committee on Un-American Activities** to seek out, identify, and prosecute any subversive individuals or organizations for treason."

"We require a **balanced budget** and end to senseless spending."

"We want **Energy Independence** again. It doesn't make any sense at all to force America into a situation where they must purchase oil from nations that don't like us and will use our money against us. We had reached energy independence under President Thompson, but the first thing President Dufus did was shut down the pipelines and stop drilling. Why? We will talk about special interest corruption soon.

"**Defund the United Nations** until they restore fairness, certainly to the U.S.."

"We want **America first** restored. It was working."

"I think we all can also agree on the need for, **Term Limits**. Our government does not want or need career politicians that get wealthy from **lobbyist's campaign contributions**, which should also end. Lobbyist corrupt the election process and the politician by, in essence, buying votes in their favor and not always in the best interest for the U.S.."

"The founding fathers never envisioned Congressmen and Senators to rule for life. They anticipated leaders in the community and states to serve the people for one term, without pay I might add, then return to their own states to live under the laws they enacted. This leads to a secondary demand, **End Retirement for politicians.** Today we have pensions for life for politicians that serve only one term. I didn't realize that fact, and it was shocking to me of the audacity of politicians voting that law in for themselves. Any law that personally benefits the politicians, like their personal health care, raises, or retirement pensions, should be voted on as a referendum by the people. It's unfair to the tax payers without their approval.

"There are some secondary demands that can and should come about as a restored patriotic government begins to reasonably function again to serve the people. This list is far from all encompassing, and the Manifesto will only represents a few demands. If there are others we have not touched upon, and I'm sure there are, you should approach your representative in government and voice your concerns. I do believe they will be motivated to listen in the future."

"Only a few of these demands will actually make it into the Manifesto, mostly those that require immediate implementations. The Manifesto must be kept short, tell the story, and make demands. I'm passing out a copy of the draft American Manifesto. Remember, it's a first draft, so please take your time

163

to read it over and feel free to make suggestions at our next meeting."

When Dr. Wisscross finished, the audience stood and applauded, and the military delegations were the loudest. They had obviously contributed heavily toward Dr. Wisscross' contribution, and apparently they felt that he did a great job of capturing their input.

***

Mary and Jerry's team had been busy, and it had also grown. Mary had insisted on increased participation from the other Star Children in the workings of ARC. Ten additional Star Children had undergone the archive ARC training and were now proficient in the operations of ARC, especially in the use and application of the cryogenic chambers and use of the teleport and weapons systems.

Tina, the only Star Child left alive with the ability to see glimpses into the future, come to Mary with a future warning.

Tina said, "You know how we planned to use some of the NAZI soldiers to control and herd the people we plan to teleport and put them into the Underworld?"

"Yes, and use them as backup assault teams. What about them?"

Tina continued, "Do you remember how I saw Tom even before we met him, and how I saw the clues we used to find the Sanctuary?" Mary nodded. "Well, I saw something about the NAZIs in the future that scared me. In my vision they were taking over the ARC and killing some of us."

Absolutely, Mary remembered those incidents Tina spoke of, and if Tina said she saw something in the future, Mary believed her. Mary said, "Thanks Tina. I will contact the others and let them know about your warning." Tina smiled and bounced off again on her own mission, whatever that was.

With the addition of more ARC trained operators, Mary and Jerry were not required onboard all the time. They had plenty of operators to maintain continuous shifts on ARC. When Tina brought the new problem to her, she knew immediately what that meant. The war with the NAZIs was not yet over, and the Star Children needed to take precautions to protect themselves and their current Coup plans. She was about to suggest they take one of the saucers on the ship when Jerry interrupted her thoughts.

Jerry said, "Hey Sweetie, I saw you thinking and looking at the saucer storage area. I know you were about to suggest we take one of the saucers and go talk to the others. I agree that Tina's concern needs to be shared with the others, and I agree we should do this in person to see the body language and reactions, but, Hon, we don't need to go to all that trouble when we have a perfectly good teleport system, which we are currently experimenting with."

Mary smiled at Jerry, realizing he had read her thoughts correctly, and said, "Well, that is a fantastic idea. I hadn't applied those experiments toward our personal use. Let's do it."

Jerry said, "We need to have this discussion in private where General Bruner doesn't hear it. Maybe we should bring them up here."

Mary nodded and said, "Do you think we should give them a warning?" Jerry smiled and shook his head.

Mary activated the controls, located the targets within the Sanctuary, and activated the controls. Jerry quickly descended to the teleport room and watched as wide-eyed targets began to materialize within the teleport chambers. Tom and Sue came simultaneously, followed closely by John and Jane, Berta and Fred came next, and finally came a very surprised Dr. Wisscroff who stumbled and had to be caught by John as he exited the chamber.

A very distressed Dr. Wisscroff said, "What is the meaning of this?" He looked around and said, "Obviously, we have been teleported to the ARC, but why was I not warned previously. I'm a very old man. Something like this could give me a heart attack."

Tom said, "I don't think any of us was warned, but personally I probably would have been more afraid, knowing. I assume there is an important reason for this."

Jerry said, "Yes, we needed privacy for what we need to tell you and discuss. Mary is waiting for us in the Control Room." The group, plus a mysteriously appearing Tina, followed Jerry up the ramps to the Control Room, where a very attentive Mary waited.

Mary grinned at the still somewhat shocked group and said, "Sorry for the dramatics, but the

166

subject of our discussion needs privacy. It has to do with one of Tina's visions. She came to me in fear to report her vision. She said she saw some NAZIs here in the ARC killing Star Children. We all know about the accuracy of her visions, and the implications of this one is fairly obvious. We have planned to use the NAZIs as guards for those Coup targets we plan to teleport here. We also discussed using them as assault back up to the ground operation as needed. Her vision implies strongly that they plan or will plan a coup of their own. We felt we needed to discuss this here without any worry of it being heard."

Tom said, "You are right about that, for sure. If the NAZIs were able to control the ARC, they could still dominate the world with their 4th Reich. But, only a Star Child can pilot the ARC."

Dr. Wisscroff said, "Unless they forced the Star Children to participate in their coup. That's unlikely, but conceivable with leverage. They could take captive Star Children. Think about that Tom, John, Jerry. What if they held hostage your mates? You might find yourselves required to save their lives."

John said, "I'm afraid the temptation would be too great for their malevolent mindset. I must admit I didn't see that possibility coming, but now it's clear that they would definitely attempt it. They probably haven't thought of it yet, but they wouldn't be able to resist the temptation. Thanks Tina. You saved us again." Tina smiled.

"At this point, however, we can prevent it from happening by never letting them aboard the ARC.

Of course we must change our current plans. I believe we must scrap our plans to relocate those 25,000 to the Underworld." Sue cringed at the fleeting hope she had enjoyed.

Berta said, "Well, maybe not. There might be a way. I downloaded to my mine some of the archive files and have been analyzing them. As I understand, the current plan calls for teleporting some of those targeted into the ship, then escorting them to the cryogenics chambers. Right?" She got several nods. "But, possibly, once we have them in the teleport chambers, we could simply then teleport them directly into a cryogenics tube. I believe we could automate the process easily so the whole process seems continuous. The teleport chambers would only function as an intermediary stop during the dual process In this way we can bypass any need for prisoner supervision and direction, and when the targets were revived, the individuals would barely even remember the experience. At the designated time we could also teleport them into the Underworld."

Mary said, "Damn. That's a great idea. I wished someone on our team had thought of it. I guess we were just too close to the problem to see the solution. Berta, we would appreciate your help with that application." Berta nodded.

John said, "That makes a lot of sense for the internal situation, but we would still have a problem with a backup team. I suppose, however, we could get an assault team from one of the other generals."

Tom said, "I'm sure we can. I will ask General Warner. But, John, you still have the problem with the NAZIs. What do you suppose we do about that?"

John laughed and said, "We have always known that they are not to be trusted. That's why I won't let them out of the Underworld. Still, I can't punish them for something they might do in the future. We just need to make sure we don't give them the opportunity in the future and protect ourselves. I would suggest that you keep a permanent squad of Colonel Burn's Marines on the ARC to maintain security, especially in the Control Room. They are used to us and know what we are capable of. They are used to taking care of and protecting us. They are like family."

Tom said, "Dr. Wisscroff, do you have anything to add?"

"Do you mean, other than don't transport me again without warning?" Everyone laughed, even though he was not joking. "As to the other, I think Berta's application is sufficient to explain the change of plans. General Bruner might have a complaint, since it disrupted his plan or future plan, but that can be averted by General Warner asking for that change. I'm sure, after a secret discussion with him, he can come up with a good reason. John, you do know that General Bruner will require watching and probably eliminated at some point?"

John said, "I certainly do, and I will have to deal with that after this Coup is complete. I've always known how his mind works, but you will have to admit that he brought much insight and strategy to the discussions and plan that would not

169

have manifested itself without him. I knew that when I brought him in."

Tom said, "Mary, did you have other issues to discuss?"

"Well, yes I do. We have been orbiting Earth for weeks with little to do. So, we decided to analyze the satellites currently in orbit and have discovered some interesting facts. There are two large satellites with missiles and nuclear warheads. I know there are not supposed to be weapons in space, but China and Russia both have them. America is the only country that is obeying the International Treaties, and that's probably the result of the embedded Communist influence. They don't want America to have that defense."

"What would you like us to do about it, if anything? We can blow them up, but the operators would discover a threat in space and come look for us. They wouldn't find us, but they would know something exist out here and eventually presume it is us."

Tom said, "We can't let them remain operational. So, what can we do to sabotage them without being suspected?"

Jerry said, "We can't go out and disrupt them manually, because there is, I'm sure, some form of intrusion alarm, and if there is, they could detonate a self-destruct. Possibly, we could use a low dose of EMP (Electro Magnetic Pulse) focused on specific parts. This could be explained by solar flare radiation if we time our pulse to coincide with any flares, and they occur all the time. Damage could still be suspicious but explainable. I'm thinking we could also time the EMP pulses simultaneously, so if Russia and China compare notes they could reasonably conclude the same solar flare hit both. The EMP wouldn't destroy the satellite, but would cause it to malfunction."

Dr. Wisscroff said, "As an astrophysics I would come up with that suspicion, based upon those facts."

Tom said, "The bottom line is: they need to be deactivated, and I don't really give a damn how, or if we get discovered. It's probably better, however, that we don't get discovered with this other activity ongoing. I say go ahead and do it like Jerry was describing." They nodded.

***

At today's meeting Tom reported on the weaponized satellites in orbit and how he had authorized their deactivation. He also explained the changes of the ARC's participation in the upcoming Coup, that Berta had come up with an application to teleport directly into the cryogenic chambers. When he explained there would be no need to have NAZI soldiers onboard to escort the targets to the cryogenic chambers, General Warner looked pleased and General Bruner frowned.

General Warner immediately stood and said, "We will still need an assault team on the ARC to support any team problems on the ground. Might I suggest you allow me to place a team of mine on the ARC for this purpose? Our teams are trained together and accustomed to working with each other, and I prefer my own backup team." Obviously, he and Tom had spoken.

171

Tom said, "You don't seem surprised that China and Russia had nuclear missiles in orbit. I thought that would generate rage."

"It did generate rage when I first learned of it, and it still does, but we have known about them for several years. We currently have ground based lasers poised to destroy them if necessary. I am extremely pleased, however, that you have disrupted their operation. We can now retarget our lasers."

Tom just smiled and said, "From your lack of reaction, that's what I thought. As for your request for a shipboard assault team, I agree."

Admiral Jones said, "We have talked among ourselves about the American Manifesto, and we all agree that nothing be changed. It does what it was designed to do ... very well."

General Warner said, "The military is ready to move, all we have to do is give the orders. We are ready on our end of the Coup. We are planning to leave tonight to take command of field operations, but Admiral Martin will remain here as liaison. Berta was kind enough to provide a secure communication network for us to use."

Berta stood and said, "We are also ready. In fact, we have developed applications and are automated. All the targets are being tracked through our satellites and constantly updated as to their locations. This information will be automatically relayed to the Hit List teams prior to execution, these are also being tracked. The NSA teams are standing by. Our financial Hit List is ready to be executed. Mary's targets are assigned, and we have

172

developed an automatic application. Bottom line is, we are ready for our target date in two day. We have been extremely lucky that there have been no security breaches. Maybe I should say our security procedures have worked flawlessly."

Dr. Wisscroff said, "It sounds perfectly planned and, hopefully, will be perfectly executed. But, and it's a big but, no pun intended, we don't know what the world's reaction will be. There is a possibility our Coup could stir world action against the U.S. during America's perceived weakness. What are we prepared to do in that case?"

John said, "Jane and I will transfer to the ARC tomorrow to monitor the world's reaction and potential action. We have already talked about Jane's influence with Russia. We helped them when they needed it, and they owe us, should we are forced to intervene. And maybe Russia has some influence with China. At any rate, we will be standing by in the ARC. The ARC is our first line of defense for the Sanctuary, the Underworld, and our first line of offense, should that be required."

Tom said, "It sounds like we are ready to launch the Coup. This is the last chance to speak up." No one spoke up. "Very well, It's a go in 48 hours."

As everyone was leaving, General Bruner held back to catch John and Jane. As they approached the general, he waved them toward him.

General Bruner said, "Can I speak to the both of you for a moment?" They nodded and sat down beside him. He continued, "This doesn't have anything to do with the Coup. I have a personal problem with my family back in the Underworld I've been dealing with for some time. I have a grandson, that I love, that I fear will be eliminated by his peers. In our homeland that tends to happen. Outsiders and those that are different tend to be weeded out. He doesn't fit in or conform with the others. He has been bullied, beaten, humiliated, scorned, and threatened. I'm afraid next he will come up missing. Being here in the Sanctuary and seeing how the Star Children interface with each other has got me thinking that my grandson would be better off living here. I think he would be better off and certainly safer living here, after all, he is one of you."

That last statement shocked them and John asked, "What do you mean, he is one of us?"

"He is a Star Child, at least we believe he is one. He certainly looks and acts like one of you."

"My son found him in one of your crashed saucers when he was an infant. We knew of the Arcadians and had been keeping a watch on them where the saucers come out under the ice shelf. My son was on duty watching the area when the Arcadian saucer exited the water in an erratic manner and crashed down on the ice. My son investigated the saucer and found the hatch open. The Arcadian had died at the controls, my son believed of some disease. Inside was a human infant, who was brought back and raised as his own, my grandson. This is what made us realize that the Arcadians were doing genetic engineering and creating Star Children. We assume that the Arcadians was taking the last of their created

174

product out to an orphanage when he died. After that incident we never again witnessed an Arcadian saucer, not until you guys showed up. That was almost twelve years ago. So, we presume my grandson, Jeff, is a Star Child, but he has never demonstrated any of the powers you Star Children have."

Jane said, "That's to be expected. Those powers usually remain dormant until puberty, unless awakened by necessity, like in Tina's case. I myself didn't activate my powers until well into maturity."

General Bruner said, "Like I said before, I don't want him to be eliminated. By all rights he is my grandson, and I want to see him live. If that has to be here, so be it. Maybe we can still see each other."

"Another thing that surprised me was how well this Coup planning worked out. At first I didn't think humans, and especially the Star Children, had the sand to do what was needed to be done. I was wrong, and I felt good about being so much help. I wouldn't mind working on other project with these military representatives and Star Children. You are smarter than I gave you credit for. I appreciate you inviting me here."

John said, "Can you show me where the Arcadian saucer landed on our way back to the Underworld to get Jeff? We'll bring him back with us and find out for sure if he is a Star Child. If he is, he will have a home with us. Even if he isn't he can live here. Tina needs someone her own age to socialize with." The general gave them a rare smile.

General Bruner said, "I'm afraid the saucer is no longer there. My son said it exploded, and he suspected that it was some form of self-destruct initiated by the dying Arcadian."

While the general headed toward his quarters to get his gear, John and Jane proceeded toward the saucer storage area. John said, "Maybe we misjudged the general. He may have some humanity in him after all."

Jane said, "This could also be a ploy to take our minds off of the potential NAZI coup. Don't trust him and keep your guard up. I mean, why has he never mentioned before that his grandson is a Star Child? This fact could easily put us off our track."

"It is amazing, however, to possibly find another Star Child, and of Tina's age. If true, that would be great for Tina. She is the only Star Child that doesn't have a potential mate. Another thing I was thinking about: This Jeff, assuming it's true, would have the vision power like Tina that could be genetically passed on in their future children. That would be great for our future race."

"Yeah, I was thinking about those things also, and don't worry, I will definitely keep my guard up."

When they met Jeff there remained little doubt that he was a Star Child. Jeff's hair was long, but it had the color of... well almost no color, white like the all Star Children. It was almost albino white, and the eyes looked like green emeralds set in a bronze face. Yes, he looked exactly like a Star Child. Evidently General Bruner had already spoken to his son and made the arrangements, because

176

when their saucer landed, Jeff was ushered out, and General Bruner hugged him and led him aboard. It was a quick trip, and they were back in the Sanctuary within thirty minutes. Jeff was obviously nervous but not scared.

Jeff mustered up the courage to say, "This is the Sanctuary? It looks fantastic here. Will I be staying with you, Grandpa?"

"Yes, until we find out if you are truly a Star Child. It could take a few days." Jeff accepted his fate with a nod.

Their first stop was the medical clinic, where the Navy doctors drew blood for Jeff's DNA analysis. They would know for sure in a few hours, along with his current medical evaluation. Their next stop was the cafeteria where they knew Tina would be at lunch time. They didn't have to wait long. Tina saw someone her own age and came running.

Tina purred out, "Hello. My name is Tina. What's yours?"

"My name is Jeff."

"Are you a Star Child?"

"Everyone seems to think so. They are checking out my blood to make sure."

Tina giggled and pulled at his hand and said, "You look like one of us, but there are better ways to find out. Come with me. I'll have you flying in no time."

As Jeff was being dragged out by Tina, he was saying, "Flying?"

Tina said, "Yes, if you are a Star Child you will be able to do many things. These powers just have

177

to be woken up. Just forget about what you have been told about what you can't do and just do them. Like they tell you that you can't defy gravity. You can if you believe. A Star Child can control gravity with their minds, and we have big minds. When you can control gravity you can fly. Like me."

Tina slowly lifted herself in the air and floated in front of and above Jeff, who stared in total disbelief. He began quivering with the effort of trying to lift up, but nothing happened. Sweat broke out on his forehead from the effort. Jeff finally stopped trying and said, "I can't. I want to, but I can't."

To further tease Jeff, Tina shot up and began twirling in the air, then shot straight up and began an intricate display of aerobatics, that only she could do. Tina always did like to demonstrate her flying abilities and show off. While Jeff watched in amazement, she resumed her standing position.

Tina said, "I have taught many others like us to fly, like I'm about to show you. I want you to lay on your back in the grass. Now, close your eyes." He did. "Now, relax and open your mind and imagine your body is weightless. Imagine you feel me pick you up and lift you about three feet and turn you over. Imagine now that I drop you. Feel yourself fall. Now, Jeff, open your eyes."

When Jeff opened his eyes he found himself three feet in the air. He did fall after he realized where he was. Jeff said, "Damn, Tina, that hurt!"

"Yeah, but you flew. I did not lift you, you did it yourself when you thought you were falling. You only fell when you believed you should fall. You controlled gravity with your mind, so, you are a Star Child."

"Hey, you're right, I did lift myself. Wow! I really did. Now what?"

Tina laughed and said, "Now that you know you can, you believe. Just let your mind lift you up in the air."

Jeff turned his mind inward and he began lifting into the air. He smiled and began experimenting with movements. Soon he began to fly around, and Tina joined him and led him around in different maneuvers. Jeff learned fast and his confidence grew as well. They flew back into the cafeteria together within an hour.

A grinning Tina said to John and Jane and everyone else in hearing distance, "You don't have to wait for the blood test. Jeff is a Star Child."

Jane smiled back and said, "Welcome, Jeff, to your new home in the Sanctuary. We are now forty-one, and we are your family, and you are welcome." General Bruner was also smiling.

Many of the Star Children came to welcome Jeff and introduce themselves, and Jeff by now was beaming with self-pride.

Tina said, "I will teach him more of the powers as soon as I can.

Chapter 10
("D-day")

"'D-day', June 6, 1944, marked the day of the Allied Invasion of Northern France in World War II. D-day has become a catch phrase to indicate the date an important operation is to begin. The Coup D-day began Jan. 6, to be in contrast with the Communist's claim that a Coup was attempted on Jan. 6. But ... this is what a real Coup should look like.

The Coup actually began early in the evening of Jan. 5 with the launching of the designated targets from the Hit List to the designated trigger. NSA assassination orders were issued from unaware, corrupt operative, orders that could later be easily decrypted. At that time the advanced membership drive kicked off. The military readied in secret and was prepared to mobilize. ARC patrolled the sky above the U.S. and began teleporting General Warner's strike force aboard. When the strike force was aboard the ARC began snatching their specific targets and depositing them in the cryogenic chambers. Notification of the launch and instructions was sent to all Coup member categories, including two and three, the protectors and soldiers.

A later decision had been made for this timing notification change to these categories, because it was believed that if all were pre-warned they could stand down, allow access, and assist the hit teams at time of launch, less potential conflict of friendlies would occur. It was sound reasoning.

Needless to say, the archive conference room was filled far over capacity and spilled out into the halls. All wanted to watch the Coup in action and the archive met that demands by filling the wall with a marquee descriptions depicted for all categories. No huge monitor existed, just the written information magically written in the air. As an example, targets were listed as PENDING and COMPLETE, and the numbers continued to change from PENDING to COMPLETE.

The display was reminiscent of an election night news coverage. The big difference in the two was the fact that the archive data could not be hacked and manipulated like our last election.

Unexpectedly, a third column flashed on listed as COLLATERAL, which was also beginning to show advancing numbers. These were kills apparently necessary to reach a target, consisting of guards and security that had not stood down at the order. After a while longer a forth column flashed on, CASUALTIES. Apparently, some of the triggers were falling.

The volume of members in all categories began to soar so fast most of the quickly changing numbers couldn't be read. As the hours passed, the number of observers tended to float in and out of the conference room in shifts to track the changing numbers.

By 8:00 am the ARC list showed that most of the 25,000 scheduled for the Underworld had been stored in cryogenics, the Hit List was dwindling

181

fast, all the targeted funds had been seized, and the military move on Congress and the White House began in earnest. The duped NSA hit teams had taken out all their high level targets, and the NAZI cells had also completed their list.

At 9:15 am John received a call on General Warner's Strike Force duty phone, "John, we have run into a snag in our move on the White House. Most of the Capital Police stood down and left the area, but the president's special security team apparently had been carefully chosen from the corrupt. We are running into stiff resistance. I need the Strike Force team teleported behind their defense position to help take them out."

The call was on speaker, so the trained team took their positions in the ten teleport chambers, and the others lined up for their turn. Mary had located the designated battle area and selected a teleport location well behind and hidden. The force gathered then launched a coordinated attack from the rear. The surprise was total, but President Dufus' personal defense force consisted of dedicated, corrupted fanatics that fought to the death, which came in short order.

Most of the military forces locking down government facilities encountered little resistance. It became obvious that those security forces knew they were coming and unlocked and held the doors open for them. It was also like that for some of the triggers, where the security stood aside to facilitate the hit, and in some cases actually made the hit themselves.

The Strike Team had no casualties and teleported back to the ARC to await any necessary additional deployment, and the sweep of the White House continued with little additional resistance. President Dufus and his staff were arrested and escorted from the White House to a secure facility where they would be held pending a trial for treason.

The siege of President Thompson residence met with little, if any, defense, since most of his security and secret service agents were already members of the Coup forces, unbeknown to President Thompson or his inner circle.

The surprise was complete when General Warner leading that command said, "President Thompson, we are here to escort you to the White House to resume your duties as the President of the United States. There has been a Coup and you are needed again to lead us." President Thompson was so shocked, for once, he had little to say and followed along quietly.

***

The Coup was almost complete before the first major problem arose. Berta said aloud, "Russia has learned of the Coup in progress and is preparing to attack America to launch a Coup of their own in the U.S. while the government is in turmoil. We haven't detected any movement from China as of yet. What are we going to do?"

Tom said, "Notify John and Jane in the ARC and tell them what you know so far and that they are in charge of the Russia and China battle fronts. They will know what to do."

183

When Jane got Berta's telepathic message she immediately asked Mary to find President Pramin. In seconds Jane was watching the Russian president in his office talking to his generals. Jane could watch them talk, but she couldn't hear them. Jane asked, "Can you give me audio also?"

Mary nodded and let her fingers manipulate lights in the air in front of her. Mary said, "It's a strong stretch of technology to receive and amplify the audio signal from here, but I can tap into Berta's data she is listening to from the satellites."

Suddenly, Jane was hearing the audio while watching the conversation. They were speaking in Russian, but Jane, and John for that matter, we're fluent in that language, among several others. A general was saying, "Their government is in chaos. This is our window of opportunity to destroy them."

President Praman bellowed, "We are close to taking their government over from within. We don't want to destroy our own new country. No, no nukes. All we want to do is take it over before the Chinese do. We need only to prevent their Coup from being successful."

Jane said, "Now that is interesting. Russia and China are not working in lockstep with each other. I see an opportunity in this." John began to nod in understanding.

President Praman continued, "Maybe we can disrupt their Coup by launching an EMP attack to shut down their electrical grid. Turn their lights and communications off and activate some embedded cells to disrupt the Coup and protect our operatives."

John said, "I've heard enough. We have got to interfere with their plans. What do you suggest?"

Jane grinned and said, "Well, first we need to notify Berta to hack Russia's data and locate those cells the president was talking about. I think we could do with them like we did with the NSA hit teams, send them some targets that can be traced back to Russia. Let Russia answer to the world for their assassinations. Of course, the targets should have to be high level Communist targets, and since Russia and China seem to be in competition with each other for control of America, Russia would have to answer to the world and to other Communist countries. Next, I think we should teleport President Pramin up here in front of his generals for a chat."

Mary grinned and John laughed out loud, then said, "Jane, I like the way you think, and General Bruner would be jealous of your devious mind." Jane laughed. When they communicated their plan with Berta they detected exuberant agreement.

Berta telepathically said, *"I will get right on that, and I already know the targets. We have not touched the Supreme Court, since that would draw far too much attention. But, if Russia took out a couple of corrupted Supreme Court justices, they would draw the ire of the world toward them and away from our Coup."*

John said, *"Both you girls are developing devious minds."* Both telepathically pinged their acknowledgement and agreement.

President Pramin was still talking when he, chair and all, began shimmering into existence in the Control Room of ARC. At first they thought he might pass out, but the president just starred around the Control Room in obvious panic. Recognizing John and Jane, he finally said in perfect English, "What the fuck!"

Jane said, "Good morning, President Pramin. We wanted to have a private meeting with you, thus your invitation. Welcome aboard our Mother Ship, the ARC. As you can see, our powers have grown exponentially, but I hope you don't force us into showing the extent of our powers."

"What do you want?"

"As you already know, America is in chaos due to a Coup in progress. What we want you to do is stand down on your current attempt to meddle in America's politics. What you have planned will kill millions of innocent people, and we can't allow that. The Star Children will intervene to prevent that from happening."

President Pramin said, "So now the Star Children will take over the world?"

"Of course not. We are here to save the world if we can. We are always on humanity's side. After all, didn't we save Russia? Surely you haven't forgotten that small feat. Didn't John risk his life to save you from the NAZIs? Why would he do that if we wanted world control? No, we just want to protect humanity, not control it. We ask only that you stand down and let the American Coup play out to its conclusion."

"Why would I want to do that when we are so close to winning?"

"OK, let me put it another way. We will not allow nuclear or EMP weapons be launched against any segment of humanity that will kill millions of humans. We will instantly destroy them, along with the countries' controlling government. I believe you know we can and will do it. You also know we can find you anywhere you hide." The president didn't respond.

"The second thing we want you to do is scrap all your plans for the release of a weaponized Smallpox virus. Even for you, the use of bioweapons to kill off billions of people is horrific. We cannot allow that to happen, and we will intervene."

President Pramin visibly cringed at the mention of a Smallpox virus and said, "Hey, wait, that idea and plan is not coming from the Russian regime. That's totally the Chinese's plan. Our involvement is only for our own protection for a vaccine."

John said, "Well, we want all your involvement stopped immediately. We want Russia vulnerable like the rest of the world, and we want you on the side of humanity. This is your only chance to do the right thing."

President Pramin, after a moment of serious reflection, said, "I believe you mean what you are saying, the good and the bad; and Russia will comply with your requests … demands. But, understand this, by breaking with China we also become their target. Will you protect Russia in your overall quest for the salvation of humanity?"

Jane had to laugh. As President Pramin's interpreter, she had seen him negotiate terms many

187

times, and he reverted back instantly to his training, never agree to anything without getting something in return. Still, his request was reasonable.

Jane said, "As long as you're working on behalf of humanity and the people, we will be on your side. We are moving against China next. Would you like to witness our discussion?" President Pramin smiled hugely, giving his answer.

"John, as we travel, you might want to download the Chinese language, Mandarin I believe."

President Pramin said, "Chairman Chee is fluent in English. That's how we communicate." John nodded.

John said, "Mary, before we bring Chairman Chee up here, I think we need to identify China's storage and research facility for the Smallpox virus. Maybe I should first ask if ARC or our satellite lasers will destroy the virus."

Mary thought and said, "Yes, as long as we know it exists at a location we can use a wider beam and keep it active longer to make sure nothing escapes. The soaring temperatures with a wide beam will definitely kill any virus that escapes from its source."

"Great! Now can you find China's Chairman Chee?"

"We already have. He's in his office. I'm bringing him in now."

A very surprised Chairman Chee materialized within the Control Room. He blinked continuous for several seconds, as if trying to clear his lying eyes. After realizing what he was seeing was real, he said in perfect English, "What is the meaning of this? Why ... how did you bring me here?"

John said, "We are Star Children. I'm sure you have heard of us and that we have certain powers and advanced technology. We are the descendants of the Arcadian race, and we are friends of humanity. We do not normally interfere with Earth's governments unless it threatens humanity. China has and is providing that threat to humanity. Your government developed and released the COVID virus and killed millions just to attempt a Communist takeover of America's politics. This cannot be tolerated, and your current plans to release a weaponized Smallpox virus in a second phase to your takeover plan requires our intervention. Your plan has come to an end, and how far our intervention goes is up to you."

Chairman Chee panicked at the reference to COVID having been released and jumped to his feet at the mention of Smallpox virus. He bellowed, "That is a lie. We didn't release any virus, and we have no plans to release more. Just check with the World Health Organization."

John said, "WHO? You mean that organization China already controls? I guess you would be able to control them with all the money you give them. I'm sure the world would like to see those finical records and volumes of secrete communications China has given them over the years." Sudden surprise and panic flashed on his face. "There are no secrets from us. We know everything or can find it, and the world should know it too." Perspiration began flowing down his face.

"Mary, has Berta provided the coordinates of the research and storage lab in China where the Smallpox virus was developed and is stored, and is she positive it's the only place it is stored?"

Mary said, "She is positive, but she provided several other locations where China is working on other bioweapons. She also provided the ones in Russia, and believe it or not, at the World Health Organization in Geneva."

"Well, let's start with the main one in China."

The visuals materialized in the air above the control panel, as Mary flicked her fingers within the various lights. The image zoomed in to show a large building that suddenly flared white with heat for a prolonged period of time. When the image cleared there was nothing there but a deep hole with charred earth at the bottom. The building and all that was within were simply gone.

John said, "Chairman Chee, I believe you had an industrial accident at one of your scientific facilities. Shall we continue our discussion?"

Chairman Chee flared red with anger and said, "We're going to blow your asses up in this fancy spaceship and will destroy your Sanctuary. Yes, we know where you are, and you're not the only ones with lasers. We have Earth based and satellite lasers that will make short work of you for us. You have no idea of our capabilities. You have messed with the wrong people." President Pramin remained silent, not taking sides.

John calmly smiled and said, "We do not respond well to threats. We require compliance

190

instead. We aren't asking much, just stop your diabolical aggression on humanity."

"Mary, we have been challenged. Please find their Earth side lasers and their satellite lasers he claims they have."

It took only a few moments before she said, "They have no satellites with laser capabilities and only one Earth based laser powerful enough and capable of firing into space. China did have a satellite with nuclear capabilities, but we have already disabled it, along with Russia's and America's weapon satellites. Yeah, I know they said they didn't have one, but we found one. We felt it only fair to maintain a balance of power. I have the China coordinates loaded." Again, the visual zoomed in on a remote facility.

"Is this the facility you were talking about?" He didn't wait for an answer and slid his finger across his throat, indicating Mary to fire. Again, the image flared and the facility disappeared. "China is having a lot of industrial accidents today. Shall we continue? We can start on your military or aircraft carriers if you like." President Pramin cringed up his face learning their satellite had been discovered and disabled, but he said nothing.

Chairman Chee lost his anger and began to see the reality for what it was. This was a battle he could not win, and his bluff had been called. He said, "What do you want?"

"As we have already said, stop your diabolical aggression on humanity. We aren't trying to take you over or even interfere with China's government. We are simply intervening in your attack on humanity. Billions will die at your hands, and it can't be allowed to continue. Will China comply with our requests?"

Chairman Chee said, "China will comply. Now stop destroying our facilities. They are our country's defense"

"Oh, sorry, but didn't you just threaten to blow our asses up with those defense weapons?" Chairman Chee just hung his head.

"Thank you, Chairman Chee. Now I'm informing both President Pramin and you, chairman. America is experiencing a military Coup at this time, probably one that you both caused. We request that both of you stand down from interfering with its due process. We are here to ensure this outcome. You should know that the Sanctuary does have advanced technical capabilities that you seriously don't want to experience. As we have said, we are not aggressive, but we will defend ourselves and humanity. Our satellites and this ship are monitoring Earth, and our satellites *are* weaponized and operate with AI to attack automatically. We will not allow aggression in the form of nuclear warheads or EMP attacks. Those missiles will be immediately destroyed, along with the originator of the order. I tell you this in case you change your mind after you leave. Keep in mind that we can find you wherever you hide."

"President Pramin, will you comply with our requests, or do you need a demonstration also?"

President Pramin, ever clever, said, "The Star Children saved Russia and the world, I might add, from being dominated. Of course we will stand with the Star Children, our saviors."

Jane laughed out loud and said, "You are so suave, but I suspect you mean what you say this time, because you have no choice. We hope your countries will become a shining example of improving humanity on Earth. We are returning both of you to your original locations, along with your chairs. We have our own."

***

Tom and Sue had been monitoring the activities and conversations onboard ARC with President Pramin and Chairman Chee and quickly passed on the information to the assembled Coup team. Cheers rang out at the good news, and Admiral Martin, who had remained in the Sanctuary as liaison between the Sanctuary and the military, immediately communicated to the field commands that Russia and China had agreed to stand down. That was one less worry.

Berta said, "I might add that we hacked the Russian database several hours ago and Russia issued traceable orders to its embedded strike team cells in America to eliminate two of the corrupted Supreme Court justices. We refrained from touching them before due to the potential outrage, but if Russia is found to have assassinated them, the outrage will be directed toward them."

To accent Berta's statement, the marquee began to update the displayed completion numbers, with only an occasional upward change, but one of those changes registered a new category, Supreme Court Justices … two. Tom smiled, knowing of Russia's documented involvement and liability. Jane and John had done extremely well.

Tom's attention quickly returned to the marquee at the sudden cheering. The marquee announced that President Thompson was en route back in the White House and had formally accepted and resumed his position as President and Commander in Chief. And, he had declared America to be under Martial Law. For all practical purposes, the Coup was complete. They would continue to monitor the situation, but with the major Communist operatives mostly gone, there would be little resistance now.

Dr. Wisscroff got his attention and said, "Dir. Setliff is on the phone. He and Mr. Canton want to come here. What shall I tell him?"

"Tell him it took them long enough to figure it out, but that Sue and I will come get them in an hour. I assume they are still at the resort and not the White House." Dr. Wisscroff nodded. "Good. You come with us and bring your phone."

Chapter 11
(The Day After)

Dir. Setliff, Tom Canton, and Dr. Horowitz entered the archive Conference Room just behind Tom, Sue, and Dr. Wisscroff. It looked like a beehive inside. Everyone was doing something, although it was hard to identify what. But, what became immediately obvious was the information being displayed on the marquee. Dr. Horowitz actually covered her eyes, apparently subconsciously believing if she didn't see the information she wouldn't have to accept it as fact that mass assassinations had occurred. Dir. Setliff and Tom Canton actually got weak kneed and pulled a chair out to sit.

Tom Canton recovered enough to say, "Do these numbers mean what I think they mean? Has the Sanctuary resorted to assassinations en mass?"

"No, we did not do the assassinations ourselves. We just coordinated the Coup and provided the encrypted communications, and as you can see, we are monitoring the progress. But before you judge, I suggest you read the minutes of our meetings and the more detailed transcriptions, if you want more details. You can only read them here under supervision, and you will not be allowed to record any of it, for obvious reasons. If you don't then agree with our decision and actions, so be it. It won't change a damn thing, but remember you are still left with the task of helping President

Thompson move the country forward. You three were apparently sent by President Thompson, so you are part of the privileged few to be allowed to know the truth. Respect that privilege and use it to help the president. You will see that we have purposely kept the president and his closest confidants out of the knowing inner circle to give you plausible deniability. Use that deniability. You will also see the planted, hidden data and false information and investigation targets that need to be explored. Now enjoy." They were led toward a quiet corner and handed a thick printout to peruse, and each one had a Star Child watching over their shoulder.

The three were all skilled speed-readers and skimmers from their many years of high volume paperwork. Still, it would take them a while to glean the gist of the information provided. They would remain busy for several hours.

Dr. Wisscroff went back to his normal seat to continue to monitor the progress and any subsequent discussions. He was shocked to see the Hit List numbers surpassing the projected numbers by substantially higher numbers. He said, "What's with the higher Hit List numbers?"

Berta chuckled and said, "We noticed the unexpected increase while you were gone. What we have discovered is that apparently, our soaring new members didn't want to be left out of the Coup and have decided to act on their own to join in the Coup. We can't really track the identity of the triggers, but most of those taken out could have easily been on our Hit List. Of course, there are a few that don't make sense from our perspective. We figure some members simply took advantage of the chaos to settle a score for private reasons. That was inevitable."

"We identified many of the targets and can logically guess the process. Many of the MS-13 gang members across the nation were taken out, and they are a notorious international gang of murders. Their weapons of choice are machetes to kill and mutilate. We believe the U.S. Immigration and Customs Enforcement (ICE), on their own, launched teams to eliminate this scourge. ICE captures and deports many MS-13 members back to central America every year, but they return easily under President Dufus' open borders. We believe ICE saw the opportunity to solve their problem and acted. Many other targets identified seem to be habitual criminals. We assume they were the result of independent action from various law enforcement agencies."

Dr. Wisscroff looked puzzled and said, "To take out a gang it would take an assault team. With the subliminal commands, how could they organize without talking and planning?"

"We know that our Coup membership includes virtually all ICE members. They would all know about the Coup, the planned action, and its launch date. It would not be a stretch of the imagination to believe they, with like minds and common enemies, would have the same desire to eliminate that vicious gang and acted in unison as a team without actually talking about it in violation of the subliminal

197

command." Dr. Wisscroff just nodded his understanding.

The others at the conference table were following the conversations, and Tom said, "Berta, have you seen any other backfires resulting from the Coup?"

"Well, General Warner warned us that there might be protocols already in place that would be launched automatically under certain events. We searched for those preexisting protocols, and there were many, but we altered or completely disrupted most of them. As a result, most were prevented. Unfortunately, there remained some corrupt, operative leaders still alive and embedded in agencies. We detected newly issued assassination orders issued by these operatives, essentially targeting a limited reverse Coup. We followed our own protocols established in the manifesto to take out any that moves against the American Manifesto and amnesty order. Strike teams from the NSA, FBI, CIA, and a few other more secret agencies were dispatched, but we altered the targets." Berta laughed. "We sent those teams to take out those issuing the orders in the other agencies. We sent the agencies against each other, and of course left fake evidence in place for Dir. Setliff's investigators. Ironically, Dir. Setliff was on their hit list. We also dispatched manifest soldiers to protect their original target list, just in case. So, to answer your question, there have been backfires, but it was anticipated and eliminated."

Tom said, "You and your team have done a fantastic job, Berta, and it looks like you headed off complications."

***

General Warner's team led the convoy with President Thompson en route to the White House. As they traveled down Pennsylvania Ave., the President marveled at the display of thousands of waving patriots lining the side of the road on both sides wearing red hats with AM on the front. There were also many signs reading "We are the American Manifesto" with larger letters of A M on the sign - "We love you President Thompson" - there was even a banner draping over an overpass that said, "Welcome Back President Thompson".

President Thompson said, "How can this be? Something this huge takes incredible planning, organization, and time to deploy. How in the world did they know? Hell, the Coup just happened, and the Manifesto just came out a few hours ago. This is all so humbling, and I'm seldom humble." The general chuckled, knowing this to be true.

General Warner said, "You haven't seen anything yet. There are about a million patriots gathered in DC and about a hundred thousand gathered at the Lincoln Memorial hoping to hear you address them. It's like that all over the country. Rallies in support of the Coup, the American Manifesto, and you, Mr. President. I think the movement you started was and is much bigger that you realize. The vast majority of the citizens of this country wanted a Coup and expected it to happen. Actually they knew in advance but don't ask how. I

199

think that's why so many are coming out in support of it."

Even while the general made his statement to the president, he was remembering all the long hours, weeks, and months spent by so many planning, organizing, and the deployment and communication required. It was a highly motivated, massive, and a technical miracle of achievement, which unfortunately, the president may never learn, not yet anyway. But, it was needed to save America, and all the effort was worth it to him just to see President Thompson humble.

The general's exuberance ended as they came to a sudden stop at the entrance to the White House. Barricades were across the road at both entrances blocking their access. A heavily armed Army detachment stood guard behind the barricades. He wasn't quite sure how or when they arrived. It would have had to be after his troops locked down the White House. They had Marines with them in the convoy but not enough to force their way through this blockade, not without a major confrontation, and they had the president to worry about. General Warner called Admiral Martin in the Sanctuary and relayed his needs.

Admiral Martin brought the Sanctuary committee the next major problem when she said, "General Warner just called with a problem for the ARC. The general is currently escorting President Thompson to the White House and he has encountered a military roadblock. He needs his strike force put behind their blockade." Tom immediately transmitted the information to John in the ARC.

General Warner, along with several of his staff and Secret Service agents, walked to the barricade and demanded to see the commanding officer, who promptly came forward. A full Colonel walked out to face him.

General Warner said, "You are blocking President Thompson's entrance to the White House. Let us pass immediately!"

The colonel said, "Sir, I was ordered directly by General Milford to come and block Mr. Thomson's entrance at all cost." General Milford must have believed that if President Thompson wasn't able to get into the White House, he couldn't assume office.

"Colonel, do you know who I am? Can you see the four stars on my collar? General Milford has only two stars. I am his superior officer, and I'm giving you a direct order."

"Sir, Yes Sir, but I have my orders, which must be obeyed."

General Warner smiled and said, "I countermand those orders."

"Sir, you know I must obey those orders unless they are countermanded by General Milford himself."

"I'm afraid General Milford can no longer give orders. He is dead and no longer in command. Again I command you to stand down, now! And, before you respond, please look over your shoulder."

General Milford, by his corrupt status, was a poster boy for the Communist operatives in politics. He had been placed high on the Hit List, but he had been well protected, and it took a highly proficient sniper to finally take him out. Evidently, it was a second or third attempt that finally got to him. So, he had managed to live long enough to have issued these orders to the colonel, and the general's White House, lockdown detachment had thought the colonel's blockade was part of them. That mistake was quickly corrected by Admiral Martin while the general and colonel talked. Many of the general's original team now stood with guns aimed, behind the colonel's troops, along with General Warners' strike team from the ARC plus some quickly dispatched Capital Police and Secret Service. When the colonel turned to look, he realized he and his detachment had no chance.

The colonel turned back to the general and wisely said, "Sir, Yes Sir. We are standing down," He saluted smartly and ordered the barricade opened for the new president to pass.

General Warner said, "Thank you, colonel. Maintain your blockade and report to my command in the White House."

When he returned to the president's limo he said, "That was a close one, but it worked out well. No one died."

After President Thompson was allowed to pass the barricade, he was quickly escorted into the White House. They're waiting for him inside was the Chief Justice of the Supreme Court ready to take the oath of President Thompson. Under normal circumstances this would be a major ceremony, but this was just as legal, according to his legal counsel. There were media there, but President Thompson recognize few of them. The missing glaring and snarking media nemesis he always had to deal with were pleasantly absent, to which he was thankful.

It was a quickly administered oath of office, and it actually angered him when he repeated the oath for the second time, knowing how the last couple of presidents, not him of course, took this oath and blatantly lied to the American people.

("I do solemnly swear (or affirm) that I will support and defend the Constitution of the United States against all enemies, foreign and domestic; that I will bear true faith and allegiance to the same; that I take this obligation freely, without any mental reservation or purpose of evasion; and that I will well and faithfully discharge the duties of the office on which I am about to enter: So help me God.")

He thought, *"How could they swear to defend the Constitution of the United States, when they tried to destroy the Constitution at every turn, and how could they defend against enemies foreign and domestic when they were the enemy?"*

***

It took many hours of illuminating speed-reading and skimming to review the minutes of the many planning and discussion meeting held there in the Sanctuary archive conference room, and all of them at one point or another had expressed outrage or praise out loud verbally. As the three-person group individually completed their study, they remained silent awaiting the other's final closure of the printout.

When Dir. Setliff finished, the last one to close the document, Dr. Wisscroff, Tom, and Sue came over to join them.

Dr. Wisscroff said, "Now you know what we know and what has been accomplished, none of which you can reveal. It's enough to know why and how. What are your comments?"

Dr. Horowitz was the first to speak, already waving her hands, said, "I can't believe what the corrupted officials have accomplished in the decades that have passed. Actually, I can believe it, as I have seen most of it during my lifetime. I just never realized it happened until I saw it all spelled out, and I would never have believed it got as bad as it has. The orchestrated release of the COVID virus and planned release of Smallpox sold me for sure. Honestly, in your shoes I would have agreed with all that has been done, and that surprises me. You have accomplished a masterful feat, and I'm thankful that you kept us out of the loop on this. It's now our turn to take the reins of this beast, which we will now do."

Tom Canton said, "I agree with Dr. Horowitz. Masterfully done, and considering the alternative, I would also have reluctantly agreed to the method, and I'm sure President Thompson would have also. But, you know he could never publicly acknowledge or agree with the method. Thanks for keeping him excluded. It will help him now."

"Is this," pointing, "marquee displaying Coup membership really accurate? It shows more Coup members than those that actually voted for President Thompson, well that were counted anyway."

The membership numbers continued to spin on the marquee and hadn't seemed to slow all afternoon. Membership had grown to over 80,000,000 and still rising.

Berta, hearing Tom's question, said, "Oh yes, and far more accurate than the manipulated vote totals. The numbers have continued to increase even more since the Coup. We are assuming the original members began to give out the phone number. As you now know, the original members were ordered to maintain secrecy, but that order disappeared on the day of the Coup … today. These new members have to make an effort to become members, and I might add, even the new members are vetted. Apparently they want to be members for them to find or obtain the number and call. Of course, anyone or activity seeking to identify the origin of the number will find a perpetual endless list of dead end routes."

Dir. Setliff said, "Who wrote the American Manifesto? It is a stroke of brilliance that was needed, and the timing and distribution was perfect."

Dr. Wisscroff said, "Thank you. I did the wordsmithing, but it came to life as a joint effort and collaboration of many people after long discussions."

Dir. Setliff said, "As you well know, I will inevitably become the new FBI Director under President Thompson and resume where I left off, as soon as I replace the now vacant positions. You have given me many new directions to investigate, but I will require substantial evidence to prosecute. You have obviously hacked and obtained much of what I need, but I must have reasonable cause to legally investigate and hard evidence for that purpose. The new Attorney General, whom I presume will be Mrs. Horowitz, and a newly rebuilt DOJ must quickly conduct investigations and convene several Grand Jury cases. To do that we need access to the data you retrieved."

Berta said, "All the evidence will be provided to you, in fact we will give you access to all our finding. If that's not enough, we will provide you with access codes for you to use to reach the original source. We can absolutely provide you with all the data, or we can get whatever you need. As to the reasonable cause concern, we can anonymously leak certain damning documents to the media that will generate alarming headlines. These news stories would force the public's demand for an investigation. Am I right?" Dir. Setliff just shrugged in thought and then nodded.

Dr. Horowitz said, "Convening a Grand Jury will also get us abundant media coverage to let the citizens know our targets are being pursued, and at this point, the media is without their leftist leaders that tend to silence the real news. Grand Juries are supposed to be held in secret, but I have never known one that was. Also, Dir. Setliff, we must remember that most of those we plan to go after are no longer among the living, therefore there will be little resistance from them. It will, however, provide an information route to the public to justify many of the targets and support the manifesto, which appears to be the focus of the Coup right now. Most members seem to be focusing on the ideology of the manifesto and not necessarily on President Thompson himself. This, I think is good for all concerned, but it does tend to alter the perspective of our future actions. We should focus our attention on satisfying the public demands of the manifesto, and not necessarily supporting President Thompson, even though he will be the one leading the action. He always has been the driving force of the movement, and the people know that. By focusing on the manifesto it will appear that President Thompson is being led by the manifesto and separate him from any personal dislikes or opinions."

Dir. Setliff said, "Yeah, I agree that that might be the best approach and will advise President Thompson accordingly."

"Tom, I am happy to hear about the recovery of the Mother Ship. It would have been a strong asset during the Alien War, but at least you have it now. I was intrigued to read about all the improved and advanced technology as well, especially the ability to teleport. You used it well with Russia and China. I had worried about their involvement and read the longer transcript of the conversation onboard the ARC. Please give my compliments to John and Jane. They did well. Mr. Canton did you already know about the nuclear warheads in orbit that they deactivated?"

NSA advisor Canton said, "I was also interested in that part. We suspected they did, but had no way to confirm it. That's why we put our own satellite up, which I'm sad to read has also been disrupted. But, we had no idea about the ground based laser. I'm glad that's gone, too. It could have taken out our satellite, which now they don't have to do, or can now. I wish none of us had nuclear capabilities."

Berta, always listening and seeking new challenges, said, "Now that's an interesting idea. I'm wondering if it is possible to neutralize uranium so that it's atoms doesn't split. That would neutralize nuclear weapons. I will check with Mr. Mum and research that possibility."

Tom, genuinely surprised at her statement, said, "It would be fantastic not to have nuclear weapons at all. If you can pull that off I'll come over there and kiss you."

"Sorry, Fred is the only one I allow to kiss me." Fred just grinned, and the others laughed.

Dir. Setliff said, "Damn, Tom. We want her to do it, so don't threaten her." Everyone within hearing range laughed.

Admiral Martin broke up the laughter when she said, "General Warner is looking for you three. They need you back at the White House quickly. I didn't tell him you were here. No one needs to know that."

Dr. Wisscroff sported a mischievous grin and said, "Berta, can't we make the trip for them quicker and more interesting? The admiral said they wanted them there quickly."

Berta gave him a knowing smile and said, "I do believe we *can* speed the trip back to D.C.."

After a few moments the bug-eyed three began to shimmer then materialized inside the Oval Office. One second they were staring at the marquee in the Sanctuary, and the next moment they were standing in front of a shocked President Thompson. General Warner literally jumped out of his chair, before he realized what had happened. Luckily, President Thompson and the general were the only ones in the Oval Office at the time, but of course Mary knew that before the teleportation.

General Warner, said, "A little warning next time might be helpful. We don't want anyone else to see what just happened. They would certainly know that the Sanctuary had involvement in the Coup. That must remain a secret." He winked and said, "We can't explain to the Secret Service how they got here, so there will be more rumors about your secret entrance."

Dr. Horowitz laughed, winked back, and said, "Yeah, that secret entrance you use to sneak your lady friends in."

President Thompson said, "Well, hell. I'd like to know what just happened."

General Warner said, "Mr. President, there are many things that haven't been told to you, but you are far better off not asking or knowing right now."

"Very well. Well, what can you three tell me?"

Tom Canton said, "As General Warner has said, there are things that you should not know to be able to maintain plausible deniability, but what you should know is that the vast majority of the citizens in this country are 100% behind the American Manifesto and through it, you. Even those that didn't like you before are now behind you as a result of the manifesto. It said what they believe needs to be done, and it said what you have been preaching. The manifesto is the result of the movement you began and pushed. It belongs to you, but we encourage you to get behind the manifesto and let *it* become your brand. That will take you further than standing alone. I say this because I have seen the membership numbers of the Coup and it is larger than the vote you received. Mr. President, these are patriots that actually joined and signed up as soldiers, and you should also know that it is not that easy to join. They are heavily vetted."

"That's amazing, but I can't very well say that can I? I wish that fact was available to the public. I could claim a mandate ... a mandate authorized by the American Manifesto."

General Warner said, "Maybe that can be done. Let me make a call."

"That would be great news."

Dr. Horowitz said, "We all agree with what Tom has just said, and what the general just said is a good idea. On the legal side of this I can also tell you that we returned to DC with volumes of evidence that we can leak to the media and many individuals and corporations, not already eliminated, that we can prosecute. We anticipate little opposition, massive public support, and maximum convictions."

"That's great, since you will be our new Attorney General, and Dir. Setliff you will head up the FBI as before. I need people I can trust. Tom, I also want you close like before as my National

Security Advisor. But, I still have to develop a staff and Cabinet. General Warner's team is working on finding and bringing back as many of my personally chosen, previous staff. That's why he was searching for you three. While we are handing out kudos, I want you, General Warner, to be my Secretary of Defense. I know being Chairman of the Joint Chief is a prestigious job, but I need you running the whole military show at the Pentagon and everywhere."

General Warner said, "Sir, I'm still active duty. I think I need to be retired for seven years before I can be nominated."

"Well, we are under Martial Law. I don't need to get a waiver from Congress, and I don't believe that would be a problem with the new Congress at any rate. Do you? I can do anything I want. Will you serve?" The general humbly bowed.

General Warner said, "What about the Vice President? Do you want us to find him?"

"Oh hell no! I don't want that idiot back. He folded like an accordion under pressure. I want to fill my Cabinet posts with great patriots this time that actually want to work for the people and in the best interest of the country. I want a VP like myself … with balls enough to fight *with* me and for what's right for America even after I'm gone. I like the governor of Florida, Desoto. See if he is interested. I might also consider Sara Balin, the past governor of Alaska and VP candidate with McWayne."

Tom Canton laughed and said, "She doesn't fit the bill. She doesn't have balls."

President Thompson also laughed, but said, "Don't kid yourself. That lady is smart and has a brass set of balls, bigger than most of those in Congress. I liked her and the way she fought during the campaign. Unfortunately, the campaign reigned her in far too much. They should have let her loose. I had to vote for McWayne with my nose pinched, but Sara had my vote right from her acceptance speech. Actually, she should have been at the top of the ticket. I want her involved in this administration in some capacity. See if she will serve."

"I'll make the calls. Also, you now have two slots open in the Supreme Court that you need to fill."

President Thompson said, "That's right. Any suggestions?"

Tom thought and said, "Well, you still have your published list, and you mentioned Cruise at the last vacancy."

General Warner looked surprised and said, "You considered an actor for a justice?" All laughed.

President Thompson said, "Not that idiot. I wanted the Texas Senator, but we couldn't take him out of the Senate, because we would have to deal with that radical O'pork trying to fill the slot."

Tom said, "The Texas governor can fill his office, plus we wouldn't have to worry about O'pork. He was eliminated in the Coup."

"Oh that's right. We don't have to make an immediate pick, since we are under Martial Law. Making my cabinet choices this time shouldn't be a problem. Right? It is my understanding that Senate confirmations will not be a problem this time, and I can make my choices based upon skill and balls and not political need." He received nods from all.

"Another thing I need to know: With all the vacancies now in the Senate and House, does our side have control of them and a quorum to pass new laws and cancel others when I give the power back? That was my major obstacle before."

Tom Canton said, "You are correct in that Senate confirmations will not be a problem, and whoever established the Hit List for the Coup, was careful to maintain quorums. The vacancies in the Senate and House happened mostly on the corrupted side of politics, which were mostly on the Democrat side but also some of the RINOs. The worst of the corrupted are gone. I suggest the vacancies remain open until a new honest election can be organized, one that can be assured to the public cannot be corrupted or stolen. The manifesto made demands in this regard, which I'm sure you already agree with."

"Of course I agree with those demands. I've been preaching on those demands for years. Oh ... I see where you are coming from. Yes, I will be happy to comply with the people's demands and support the American Manifesto. I will own it."

"I understand that there are many thousands gathered, hoping that I might speak to them and the nation. I should, and let the people hear what I have to say along with the media. General, can you let the Secret Service know, or is the Army doing security right now?"

"Your Secret Service has been vetted. Most are already members of the Coup anyway, but we will have a detachment of armed Army Special Forces with you."

The president smiled and said, "Yes, I figured that out already when my Secret Service didn't challenge you when you came to commandeer me. All of you come with me in the limo and help me make some notes for my impromptu speech."

Chapter 12
(The Speech)

Admiral Martin announced to those around the conference table, "General Warner, America's new Secretary of Defense, called and asked if there is a way to leak our marquee of Coup membership numbers to the media safely to get focused attention to how popular the American Manifesto actually is? He wants to give President Thompson some good talking points for his upcoming address to the nation."

Berta said, "I like the way he thinks, and we absolutely can do that. We can send whatever information we want to the media, and they will have no idea where it is coming from. They will also jump right on it, because it is relevant and monumental news about the Coup and not Fake News. You know, we might not stop with that. General Bruner and others presented many interesting arguments during our discussions. We could sanitize the content to hide our involvement and present it to the media. I'm thinking about the Communist Manifesto in particular that he presented along with some of his monologue. Some would take too much sanitizing. The citizens would find those persuasions as interesting and compelling as we did, and they would get major coverage, far more than the stories have ever seen in the past. We could label them as American Manifesto addendums (1 through whatever). The media and

215

public would eat it up, not to mention strengthen the members resolve."

Dr. Wisscroff said, "You know that is an incredible and intelligent idea. I wish I would have thought of it." He smiled and said, "I'm surprised I didn't. The average American, unless they are self-educated, hasn't been exposed to the hidden facts we have seen and discussed, and they need to know. And, I volunteer to continue with the manifesto addendums if that is the decision of the Assembly." Thumbs up circled the table. "Good, and since the president is looking for talking points, I think I will start with the discussion minutes of the manifesto. There are far more talking points in that discussion than were actually listed in the manifesto. I'll get that to General Warner immediately."

Tom said, "Great! I was trying to find the best way to get you involved. I think I speak for everyone when I say, 'Go for it'. And does sound like a good place to start."

"I will start immediately with the sanitizing and post my essays as addendums. By the time I'm finished, the readers will know virtually everything we know, less our secret involvement. Berta will have to show me what to do or, make the posts for me." Berta smiled and nodded.

Mrs. Wilks said, "You know, Dr. Wisscroff, you could ultimately be known as the modern day Thomas Paine. He wrote '*Common Sense*' at the beginning of the original American Revolution (1775 - 1776). The book was massively read by patriots of the 13 colonies and is considered the most incendiary and popular pamphlet of the entire revolutionary era. *Common Sense* was only 47 pages in length but presented a persuasive and impassioned case for independence. Our American Manifesto is our renewed revolution and your essays could be our *Common Sense*. Another similarity is the fact that Thomas Paine also published his work anonymously."

Dr. Wisscroff said, "How interesting. It's nice to have a history teacher around. I don't consider myself a Thomas Paine, but it does seem ironic with the similarities of the past and our current situation. It is said that history repeats itself. It certainly seems so."

Tom said, "I also find that interesting, but we need to move on."

"Admiral Martin, can you give us an update on the military's operation? Have you incurred many problems?"

"Thanks for asking. For the most part it is going as planned, better than planned, actually. The Hit List has been eliminated completely and then some. The archive communications has been phenomenal. As you know, we have far more members willing to be on the strike team than we had targets. The archive even doubled up on some of the list, just in case, and cleared the way by notifying members in each area of the pending strike. Law enforcement stayed clear, and in some cases it was the law enforcement themselves that made the designated hit."

"You may not be aware of this fact, but there were many female patriots that joined the hit team. We had one death case where the girlfriend of one of the leaders of an anarchy group hit him on the head with a cast-iron skillet. She claimed self-defense and was released by the responding police officer and fellow Coup member. Many fatal accidents, accidental poisoning, and lots of suicides were reported by maids and housekeepers. Yes, women were very active participants."

"Most of the more difficult hits, mostly politicians with security, were accomplished by NSA hit squads. The two Supreme Court Justices were taken out by Russian hit teams. Both operations of course will be investigated and confirmed by the FBI. Many others were accomplished by teams from the hidden NAZI cells, but the vast majority of the targets were accomplished by the Coup members. Many of the Coup members requested targets by name. We tried to accommodate their requests. These last two groups will not be investigated."

"The Coup military operatives have firm control of the military, government, and law enforcement. We have had little resistance due to a multitude of entrenched Coup members everywhere, and there is massive support from the citizens through rallies, marches, and demonstrations all over the country. Due to this massive support and absence of the corrupted reporters and producers, the media is now coming around to support the Coup ... well, manifesto. The anarchy groups are all but nonexistent. Some tried to organize and protest and riot, but they were quickly put down by the military and/or Coup soldiers. When I say put down I mean six foot down."

"At this point I'm saying the Coup is complete. From this point on it is in the hands of President Thompson."

***

President Thompson motioned that he was ready to go to the rally, and the Secret Service scrambled to get him into his Beast or Cadillac One, the tank as some called it, but it was designed to looked like a limousine. He didn't know how they managed to get him to the Lincoln Memorial through the thick crowd, but somehow they managed.

While en route a smiling General Warner handed the president a freshly printed document and said, "Mr. President, look what the media just published." It was a printout of the American Coup marquee showing Coup membership numbers. The membership numbers were divided into the four categories with a description of the duties expected from each category. Absent were the actual assassination numbers, which under the circumstances seemed prudent. President Thompson returned the smile.

General Warner also handed him another document and tongue-in-cheek said, "You just received this from the Coup administration, whoever they are. They're not signing anything and remaining invisible, but the caption reads, <u>Minutes of the American Manifesto Discussion.</u>

The note also says 'We heard you needed talking points for your speech. This will provide

219

additional talking points. This will also be delivered to the media for release to the general public.'"

President Thompson began reading and said, "This is great stuff I can use." Also tongue-in-cheek he said, "I hope someday we can find out the organizers and operators behind this Coup so we can thank them properly." He quickly turned back to reading the document.

They finally arrived, and the Special Forces split the cheering crowd and gave him a corridor to maneuver to a quickly placed podium complete with the presidential seal. A sound system had been installed … just in case, but there were no teleprompters or extra trimmings. The teleprompters would be useless anyway, since the president would be speaking adlib. President Thompson remained standing for many long minutes, while the rambunctious crowd cheered. Finally, the crowd quieted enough for him to speak

The president hadn't been given time to change, so he was still dressed in casual clothing of a polo shirt and slacks and not in his typical dark suit and red tie. He was, however, wearing a large, dark, dress overcoat to fight the January chill. Even though his polo shirt could easily be seen.

President Thompson said, "I want to thank you all for your support." The crowd interrupted him with cheers again. "I was surprised by the American Manifesto, apparently not as surprised as most of you were. The Army commandeered me at my Florida resort and escorted me to the White House. I was asked if I would serve as president, and I said that I would." Again the crowd cheered. "Now I'm here to tell you and the world that I will humbly honor the will of the people according to their terms outlined in the 'American Manifesto' and will serve as your president again and will build an administration that will serve the people and our country and together we *will* Make America Great Again." It took many, many long minutes before he could continue.

"I guess the patriots of America decided we couldn't wait out the term of this idiot, Communist president until the next election and took joint action. Maybe they didn't trust the next election would be honest. We have just witnessed and are participating in our second revolution and the birth of a renewed United States. Happy birthday USA. Apparently this revolution lasted only a couple of days. The loss of life is significant but far less than an open civil war lasting years would have resulted in."

"Out of necessity we are currently under 'Martial Law' and the military is running our country until I have a working Cabinet and Staff. The military has advised me that they will defer to my leadership once my administration is operational or at such time as I desire. That will be as soon as possible."

"I just came from the White House, where I was administered the oath of office, my pledge of allegiance to the United States, our Constitution, and the people I now serve." President Thompson stopped and looked around on the stage in all directions and bellowed, "Speaking of Pledge of Allegiance, where is our flag? How can we have a gathering of so many dedicated and loyal patriots without our flag? Someone, please, find a flag and bring it to the stage." He waited for many long minutes, but soon a flag could be seen fluttering above the crowd as it maneuvered through it toward the stage. A Marine came running up the ramp waving old glory vigorously amid a roaring cheer from those gathered.

President Thompson stood to attention with his hand over his heart as the flag passed. Once the flag was stationary, being held by the Marine, he said, "Let's pledge our allegiance."

"I pledge allegiance to the flag of the United States of America and to the Republic for which it stands, one Nation under God, indivisible, with liberty and justice for all."

"Think about the actual words and the true meaning of this pledge. This is our outward witness of our vow of loyalty to our country and our Constitution guaranteeing our republic ruled by its people. If a citizen of our country has a problem with loyalty to it, I question whether they should be a citizen. If you are not with us, you must be against us. The same goes for the playing of our National Anthem and desecration of our flag."

"This is the reason I'm against some of our athletes taking a knee during our national anthem. It shows disrespect to our country and all the loyal citizens. I was also offended by one of our recent, past presidents who refused to respect our National Anthem by placing his hand over his heart. I never forgave him for that contempt and couldn't respect him afterwards."

"As your president I will see these things change, along with many other treasonous acts."

"Most of you here probably haven't yet seen the latest American Manifesto information just released. I saw it on my way here. I don't know where it is coming from, I assume from the manifesto information center, wherever and whomever that is; but you can most likely see it on your news source on your smart phone. It claims that there are over 80 million members of the American Manifesto and still growing. That is more members than actual votes for me in the last fraudulent election. Well, that is more than the recorded votes in the last, fraudulent election. I am advised that this is an extremely strong mandate for me to continue doing what I do. I am honored to be requested, no drafted, to serve you and America. This I will do with renewed enthusiasm."

Some cheers rang out, but most were frantically scrolling through their phones looking for or reading the manifesto news release. After a prolonged time, a low chorus of shrieks began to grow into a crescendo as more and more gathered and absorbed the information.

"The news release says there are more manifesto releases to come in the days ahead. I will definitely watch for those releases, and I suggest you do also."

"Now! What am I going to do with your strong mandate?"

"The very first demand listed in the American Manifesto requires a general amnesty for all participating manifesto members in the course of implementing the Coup. I have vowed to honor the will of the people, and I will. Still, the United States is a country of laws, and we must not be lawless. Now that the Coup has been successful we must now return to being a country ruled by laws and justly enforced."

"The first thing I'm going to do as your president is repeal every Executive Decision enacted by President Dufus and every law enacted signed by him during his illegitimate partial term in office, with exceptions determined only by a new representative Congress, should there be any of his laws worth keeping. We will return to our Constitution of the United States of America as our sole ruling authority, and that includes the 2nd Amendment" A loud chorus of cheers rang out. "Had the Communist been successful in eliminating the 2nd Amendment and taking our guns, the Coup would never have happened."

"I intend to establish fair and honest elections as dictated by the American Manifesto. At a minimum, I will ask our new Congress to establish federal laws requiring Mandatory Voter ID; Eliminate corruptible Voting Machines, and Revert to Paper Ballots."

"I intend to establish an honest and independent Voter Integrity Agency whose job it will be to investigate and prosecute voter fraud and to certify elections. I'm considering getting the Supreme Court more involved in this process to force them, as the third branch of our government, into making rulings in a timely manner on elections."

224

"Under changes necessary to ensure fair and honest election, Congress must establish

Campaign finance laws designed to eliminate special interest groups from buying votes. Part of a solution requires Term Limits be imposed. We want our Congress more worried about doing the people's work than getting re-elected."

"Going along with this line of thought, our representatives should not be career politicians. We want them going to Congress to represent their states and its people, then going back home to live under the laws they create. One pet peeve I have: There should be no paid retirement for politicians, certainly after only one term. I not sure how they were able to get this done. Well, I do know … *they* voted it in, along with their raises and special medical insurance. I will change all that by requiring any change benefiting only politicians be voted on by referendum of the people. No entity should be in control of their own benefits. That's like letting the fox watch the henhouse. Oh well, there is a lot more I could say about this subject, but it can wait for now."

"I will insist that our already existing immigration laws be immediately enforced, and any necessary changes to those laws be enacted. And, of course, finish building the wall." Cheers rang out.

"We want a Free and Honest Press and Big Tech.. I will ask our new Congress to pass legislation making the media and Big Tech. legally liable for what they report or censor. We all saw how Big Tech promoted the left and censored the right. This has to end and will."

"We have to control our spending. I want legislation to force Congress to establish and live within a balanced budget. We have to run our country like a business. I will ask Congress for a Line Item Veto to eliminate frivolous spending on things we don't need or even make sense. Our laws passing through Congress contain far too much pork spending we can no longer afford."

"We will stop Critical Race Theory, political correctness, and WOKE in all forms and get back to a reasonable and common sense approach to life. Certainly it doesn't belong in our schools. Schools should be about teaching the basics of reading, writing, history and arithmetic and not indoctrinating our children with a Communist agenda. When I say history, I'm talking about real history, not the rewritten anti-America history invading our school curriculum. This brings me back to school vouchers. I will push our new Congress to approve school vouchers to provide an alternate method of education and competition to the looney tunes public education. Let's see who can educate our children best."

"I have no script for this speech, which means I'm talking about things my mind brings forward, and looney tunes is one such item. I used the words and it brought to mind one of the stupidest things I've seen. How many of you have ever watched a Looney Tunes cartoon of Elmer Fudd? I see many hands raised. I used to watch Elmer Fudd as a child, and he was always hunting the *wascawwy wabbitt*, Bugs Bunny. Elmer always carried a shotgun when he hunted Bugs Bunny. Have you seen the altered

226

cartoons after the WOKE crowd got hold of them? They took his shotgun away and replaced it with an axe. Now that's looney tunes, but I guess gun control ideology can never come too soon for WOKE. I'm not aware of anyone ever claiming they got the idea to shoot another because of watching Elmer Fudd cartoons. That's how insane WOKE has become. I call it 'With Out Knowledge Extremist' It must end."

"Abortions! The subject of abortions will require a lot of discussion among the states and federal government, but at a minimum I will demand an end to late term abortions immediately. If a baby can live on its own, then an abortion is murder in my opinion. Let's start these discussions from a reasonable position."

"Oh, I could go on and on. There are a multitude of other items that needs to be addressed, and maybe now we can tackle them. I just wanted to share a few of them with you. I'm told that there will be additional information about the American Manifesto demands forthcoming. I've seen some of them, and I feel confident that I will comply with those demands of the people."

"As you can surmise, there is much that I need to be doing right now, and I need to cut this short and get to work. But, I wanted to thank you again for giving me the opportunity to work for you and America again. It will make a difference."

All through the president's impromptu and unscripted speech the crowd continued to interrupt with joyous clapping and cheers, but as he finished

227

the crowd erupted in tremendous cheers that echoed through D.C., America, and the world.

Once President Thompson managed to be navigated back through the jubilant crowd and back inside his limo, he finally let his anxiety out with a bellow, "What the hell just happened? It was like I just delivered their newborn child. I've never seen a crowd like that before, and I doubt I will ever see another like it."

Tom Canton shook his head and said, "Oh, I believe you will see many crowds like that. The whole country is like that. America now has vested interest in the American Manifesto, and you started it ... hell, you *are* it. That crowd and other like crowds gathered around the country just purged America of its treasonous and criminal saboteurs and handed it back to you to manage. They are now committed to you like you have been committed to them. You have a mandate like no other president in history has ever had or could hope to have. You can now achieve all your goals and heal the nation, and it's time to get back to work."

President Thompson said, "You know, I think you are right, and I'm just now starting to realize that fact. It *is* time to get back to work. I won't let them down. Hurry, get me back to my office so I can start."

***

On the second day after the Coup the <u>Minutes of the American Manifesto Discussion</u> mysteriously appeared in the media. Every television news outlet sprang into continuous coverage and discussion, amplifying it and disseminating it to the public en

228

masse. Every newspaper carried it front page and radio talk shows discussed it ceaselessly. The public learned and wanted more, and their anger festered.

On the third day after the Coup the Communist Manifesto was released in the media and America's wrath bubbled over a second time. The resulting anger spurred the membership roles of the American Manifesto Coup to even greater heights, almost reaching 140 million members and still climbing. The resulting anger against Communist corruption boiled over, even in the media. Finally seeing the audacity of the published goals of the Communist Party, along with its accomplishments in America, opened the eyes of millions more Americans. America really woke up and became patriotic again. Even the main stream media began attacks against them and their organizations, some of which were burned down by manifesto soldiers.

The remaining anarchist groups tried to stage protest and planned some burning and looting, but as they started their protest and lit their fires and started throwing bricks at windows they were literally mobbed by patriots, while police smiled and looked the other way. In some cases the police even helped. One group of young anarchist protesters tried to intimidate and run off a group of WW-2 Vets, and that was a mistake. The elderly veterans clubbed them down with their walking canes, cheered on by the huge crowd of manifest supporters. One veteran was injured when he bit one of the anarchist and lost his false teeth.

Dr. Wisscroff continued to convert and sanitize the information forthcoming in the Sanctuary

229

meetings in subsequent anonymous news releases and essays. His goal became to educate the masses with the persuasive arguments and information the committee had undergone that influenced their decision to launch the Coup. General Bruner had been most persuasive and contributed a wealth of information. After the Coup, all the attention of a virtually massive, captive audience focused on these information releases and essays which received almost total scrutiny. America's populous soaked up the information like a sponge and wanted more, and the more they got, the madder they became. The American citizens had been duped and manipulated for decades, and they now knew it and supported the American Manifesto.

So far the involvement of the Star Children and the Sanctuary had remained undiscovered, partially because of the subliminal command, but also because the populous wanted to believe the Coup was totally enacted by American citizens. They needed to believe it was an American Coup ... a revolution ... an American Manifesto Revolution. The awakened citizens had taken back their country, and it was theirs again.

During the days following the Coup FBI Dir. Setliff and the new Attorney General Horowitz had also been successful in leaking the incriminating documents concerning the NSA involvement in ordering many of the assassinations of high level government officials including Senators, Governors, state Attorneys Generals, and Secretaries of States. These media stories were gaining traction, and without corrupt news investigators to kill the stories or spin it, public opinion was demanding action.

The identical action was also occurring concerning the Russian involvement in the assassination of the two Supreme Court Justices. Even the duped liberals were realizing how compromised and indoctrinated they had become. Russia turned inward for their own defense and salvation.

China shut down communication throughout their empire, trying to defend against the leaked evidence about their COVID Virus release and potential release of the Smallpox virus. They were not successful and had reverted to external and internal propaganda in an effort to spin the information. World opinion turned against both Russia and China, and those countries' attention reverted to self-defense, leaving America alone to work through the many changes occurring.

The media coverage of real news was returning in America and beginning to again serve the general population and not just spout propaganda, and the public was beginning to tune in again. Trust was returning and the dormant, patriotic soul of America was alive again.

***

Back in the Sanctuary things were returning to normal. The assembly had continued to monitor the situation and remained ready to get involved should problems arise, but few had. President Thompson had quickly taken firm control of the government again and had established a well running operation. The Sanctuary's involvement in the Coup seemed to have dwindled, even Dr. Wisscroff had finished with his essays. As a result, Tom felt that they could and should begin winding down their Sanctuary operation and called a meeting to discuss this fact.

Tom said, "I think we can all agree that the Coup has gone well, even better than we planned. But, the Star Children involvement is no longer needed. Obviously, the military delegation involvement is no longer required here, other than Admiral Martin remaining as temporary liaison. I thought we might meet again to update all on the progress and provide any additional comments. Since Admiral Martin is here, let's start with her."

Admiral Martin said, "Thank you Tom, and on behalf of the military and citizens of America we want to thank the Sanctuary, the Star Children, and supporters for your assistance. We came to you for help, and that's exactly what we got."

"The Coup is effective complete, and President Thompson is back in the White House and *is* in control of the government. He is developing his staff as we speak, which is what President Thompson is exceptional in doing. He is in his element now and, as we know, is good at it. General Warner is the new Secretary of Defense, Jack Setliff is back in charge of the FBI, Dr. Horowitz is the Attorney General, and Tom Desoto, the Florida governor, has accepted the position of Vice President. And, I was just notified that Sara Balin is our new Secretary of State."

"England was the first to call congratulations, but I'm also told that China and Russia have joined the rest of the world in calling President Thompson to offer their acknowledgment of his presidency and congratulations. So, the government has made the switch, and our job here is complete. Again, I Thank you."

General Bruner stood and said, "Do you mind if I speak next?"

Tom said, "Of course not. You have earned a right to speak here and our respect."

"Thank you. I wanted you all to know that I have enjoyed my time debating here in the Sanctuary and helping to develop a successful Coup. It has been a rewarding and surprising experience for me, and I am seldom surprised. I have discovered that Star Children and humans are far from the imbeciles I previously believed you to be. John tells me that I can be a real ass at times, and I supposed I can be. Still, you have treated me with respect and listened to my arguments ... even accepted most of them. I have gained new respect for those here, and I am persuaded that you *are* benevolent in nature and only want to help humanity. I was not so inclined when I came here, but I can appreciate what you are trying to do, even see the worth of it and benefits to all."

"This brings me to my next proposal and challenge to you. I can see that all involved are in the process of shutting down this operation, but I propose that you remain intact and continue to spread good will throughout the world. I mean, you have activated ARC and used it for good. It would be a shame to deactivate it again. Keep it active to police the world in secret. The world doesn't need to know you're doing it. Think about how much

233

help you could provide and how many lives you could save through your advanced technology, medical research breakthroughs, scientific knowledge, increased food production, and deterrent to war. With the power you have, you could easily take control and rule Earth, but I recognize that is not in your nature. I'm also realizing that helping humanity is almost as good as controlling and dominating it, and I, and I'm sure many others of my race in the Underworld, would want to be a part of your continued movement. It's rewarding and challenging. What do you think?" All at the table began looking at each other as if to say, "That's an interesting idea."

Sue said, "Wow! Did that just come out of your mouth? Has a change of heart come over you?"

General Bruner burst out with a rare and hearty laugh, and said, "Possibly so, but, as I have said, I have found our work here to be rewarding and challenging. I want it to continue, and you will need my somewhat radical views, views you would not consider on your own . I'm not saying you will not have to shut me down if I go too far, but I know you will listen and consider my recommendations." John seemed extremely pleased with General Bruner's remarks.

Berta said, "That is indeed an interesting idea, and I have some projects I plan to continue with anyway. One such project will be trying to find a way to neutralize nuclear explosions and rid the world of nuclear weapons. That came out of some of our discussions. That research will be extensive but profitable if we succeed. This, of course, will render nuclear power plants useless, requiring development of some of our advanced technology for power generation. That would take a while to construct and deploy … another project."

"As Mr. Mum suggested, we need to educate a Star Child in Arcadian and human advanced medical knowledge and bring in a human virologist expert to develop vaccines, certainly for the Smallpox virus, but there are many others we could research. We could find a cure for cancer, birth defects, and other deadly crippling diseases of humanity. We might also use ARC to destroy all the bioweapons in the world. That sounds like another project for ARC." Many heads were nodding.

Admiral Martin said, "Ironically, General Warner told me that he had been contacted by some of the elite military in France and Australia, both wanting to know how the Coup was accomplished. It seems they want to do the same, but have the secrecy problem they can't get around. There are probably more countries wanting to emulate America's Coup, but haven't come forward yet. He offered them no solution and played innocent, but they will figure it out sooner or later and come to us through some means. We could contact them through a shadow organization if we want to continue with our outreach."

Mary said, "I'm excited to keep ARC active, and we can do much to help the world."

General Bruner said, "See what I'm talking about? We should remain active. Just look at the projects we have already come up with, and we only just began. As I've listened I see another major project we must consider. With improved medical advances and deterrent to war we will have fewer deaths, which means we must develop a plan to combat overpopulation on Earth. This is already a real problem and must be contemplated. Even if we greatly improve food production, we have more people than can be fed. This problem won't be easy to solve. The world must enforce some form of birth control." He laughed. "I see Sue already giving me a hard stare, but you will need someone here, like me, to push hard and difficult positions."

"Sue, you had me fooled for quite a while. I thought you to be incredibly naive with your reactions and comments, until I realized you were smart and instigating me to speak my mind. I know you are doing it again now." Tom and Sue both smiled.

Dr. Wisscroff said, "Yeah, Sue does that, but she means well. Again I'm listening and thinking, and I think keeping the Assembly together and active is a fantastic idea. I have been dreaming about doing some space exploration, so I very much want to keep ARC active. Additionally, we could discuss establishing human colonies on other worlds. Yep, count me in."

Mrs. Wilks chimed in and said, "I'm with you, general. This whole Coup ordeal has been challenging and rewarding. I haven't had more fun in I can't remember when. I would love to keep our operation going, and I believe we can accomplish a lot of good and correct a lot of wrong in the world."

Berta said, "You know with our secure archive communication no one would ever know of our involvement. We could do virtually anything we want and remain hidden. We could monitor and adjust finances anywhere in the world undetected. Our archive can find and shutdown any criminal or terrorist activity. If you can control the money you can control drug cartels, any criminal activity, and governments, if necessary. Bribes can be found and reversed, and evidence can be leaked for prosecution. In short, we can wage war without armed conflict. I like the idea of staying active."

Tom said, "It doesn't sound like we need to take a vote. Let's keep it going." Nods waved around the table, and General Bruner's smile was the largest.

Phase 1 Complete

Other Books By Gary W. Babb

www.garywbabb.com

Earth is Ours (1)
Target Earth (2)
Earth's Dragons (3)

Genesis Logs (1)
Genesis Prime (2)

Star Children (1)
American Manifesto (2)
Gifted Child's Journal (3)

Apocalypse (1)
Aquatic Humanoids (2)

Dark Angels of Zeus

The People's Warrior

The Final Harvest

Bathroom Politics